Peter Bilhorn

Crowning glory No. 1

A choice collection of gospel hymns

Peter Bilhorn

Crowning glory No. 1
A choice collection of gospel hymns

ISBN/EAN: 9783337269593

Printed in Europe, USA, Canada, Australia, Japan

Cover: Foto ©Andreas Hilbeck / pixelio.de

More available books at **www.hansebooks.com**

A CHOICE COLLECTION OF

GOSPEL HYMNS,

—— BY ——

PETER BILHORN,

ASSISTED BY

A. BEIRLY.

—— PUBLISHED BY ——

P. BILHORN, 148 MADISON STREET, CHICAGO, ILL.

Y. M. C. A., 5th Floor.

✢PREFACE✢

Crowning Glory No. 1. is a collection of Songs and Hymns, for Solos, Duets, Quartettes, Chorus and Congregational singing. Especially adapted for Sunday-schools, Prayer Meetings, Revivals and Mission Work.

This work is compiled to **Herald Forth** the Gospel of our Lord and Savior Jesus Christ to a needy world, and His coming again for His people.

Yours, "Till He come,"

P. BILHORN.

☞Read carefully the notice on inside cover, and see what is said of the book.

Printed and Bound by W. B Conkey Company, Chicago.

CROWNING GLORY;

→ A COLLECTION OF →

GOSPEL HYMNS.

No. 1.

All Hail the Power of Jesus' Name!

Rev. E. Perronet, 1780. (CORONATION.) O. Holden, 1793.

1. All hail the pow'r of Je-sus' name! Let an-gel's pros-trate fall;
2. Let ev-'ry kin-dred, ev-'ry tribe, On this ter-restri-al ball;
3. Oh, that with yon-der sa-cred throng, We at His feet may fall;

Bring forth the roy-al di-a-dem, And crown Him Lord of all;
To Him all ma-jes-ty as-cribe, And crown Him Lord of all;
We'll join the ev-er-last-ing song, And crown Him Lord of all;

Bring forth the roy-al di-a-dem, And crown Him Lord of all.
To Him all ma-jes-ty as-cribe, And crown Him Lord of all.
We'll join the ev-er-last-ing song, And crown Him Lord of all.

Glory to Jesus, He Saves.

P. B.

P. Bilhorn,

1. Glo - ry to Je - sus who died on the tree, Paid the great price that my
2. Once in my heart there was sin and de - spair, Now the dear Sav -iour Him -
3. Come then, ye wea - ry, who long to be free, Come to the Sav - ior, He

soul might be free; Now I can sing hal - le - lu - jah to God,
self dwell-eth there, And from his pres - ence comes peace to my soul,
wait - eth for thee; Then with the ran - som'd this song you can sing,

CHORUS.

Glo - ry! He saves, He saves. Glo - ry! He saves, glo - ry! He saves,

Saves a poor sin - ner like me; Glo - ry! he saves,

glo - ry! He saves, Saves a poor sin - ner like me, like me.

No. 3. Come, Great Deliverer, Come.

"Thou art my help and my deliverer."—Ps. 40: 17.

FANNY J. CROSBY.

W. H. DOANE.

1. O hear my cry, be grac-ious now to me, Come, Great Deliv'rer, come;
2. I have no place, no shel-ter from the night, Come, Great Deliv'rer, come;
3. My path is lone, and wea-ry are my feet, Come, Great Deliv'rer, come;
4. Thou wilt not spurn con-tri-tion's brok-en sigh, Come, Great Deliv'rer, come;

My soul bowed down is long-ing now for Thee, Come, Great Deliv'rer, come.
One look from Thee would give me life and light, Come, Great Deliv'rer, come.
Mine eyes look up Thy lov-ing smile to meet, Come, Great Deliv'rer, come.
Re-gard my prayer, and hear my hum-ble cry, Come, Great Deliv'rer, come.

REFRAIN.

I've wandered far a-way o'er mountains cold, I've wandered far a-way from home;

O take me now, and bring me to Thy fold, Come, Great Deliv'-rer come.

No. 4. Are You Washed in the Blood?

E. A. H. Rev. E. A. HOFFMAN.

1. Have you been to Je-sus for the cleansing pow'r? Are you
2. Are you walk-ing dai-ly by the Sav-iour's side? Are you
3. When the Bridegroom cometh will your robes be white, Pure and
4; Lay a-side the garments that are stain'd with sin, And be

wash'd in the blood of the Lamb? Are you ful-ly trust-ing in His
wash'd in the blood of the Lamb? Do you rest each moment in the
white in the blood of the Lamb? Will your soul be read-y for the
wash'd in the blood of the Lamb; There's a fountain flowing for the

D. S. *garments spot-less, are they*
FINE.

grace this hour? Are you wash'd in the blood of the Lamb?
cru-ci-fied? Are you wash'd in the blood of the Lamb?
man-sions bright, And be wash'd in the blood of the Lamb?
soul un-clean, Oh, be wash'd in the blood of the Lamb!

white as snow? Are you wash'd in the blood of the Lamb?

CHORUS.

Are you wash'd in the blood, In the
Are you wash'd in the blood, In the

D.S.

soul-cleans-ing blood of the Lamb? Are your
soul-cleans-ing blood, in the blood of the Lamb?

By permission.

No. 5. Drinking at the Living Fountain.

P. H. Roblin. P. Bilhorn.

1. I have found a balm for all my woe, Je-sus is the liv-ing fount-ain;
2. When I came to Je-sus in my sin, Bend-ing at the liv-ing fount-ain;
3. As I heard his voice so kind and sweet, Sounding at the liv-ing fount-ain,
4. To the fountain come, O come to-day, Flow-ing is the liv-ing fount-ain;

I am full of joy, as Christ I know, Drink-ing at the fount of life.
Then he heard my pray'r and made me clean, Cleansed me at the fount of life.
Then I wept and sang low at his feet, Drink-ing at the fount of life.
If you come he'll wash your sins a-way, Je-sus is the fount of life.

CHORUS.

O the fount is Christ, in him be-lieve, Drink-ing at the liv-ing fount-ain;

All who come to him the life re-ceive, Je-sus is the fount of life.

No. 6. **What Will Your Harvest Be?**

Miss JULIA H. JOHNSTON.　　　　　　　　　　　　　　　P. BILHORN.

1. This is the gold-en seed-time, What will the har-vest yield?
2. Sow-ing the seeds of sor-row, Plant-ing the thorns of wrong,
3. What of your seed, be-lov-ed, You who have named His name?
4. Earn-est and faith-ful toil-ers, Bear-ing the pre-cious seed,

What is the seed, O sow-er, Dropped in the wait-ing field?
Look to the end, thou sow-er, Tho' it may tar-ry long;
Is it from out the gar-ner, Pre-cious and still the same?
Sow-ing be-side all wa-ters, Read-y in word and deed,

In-to the o-pen fur-row, Un-der the sun-light free,
Sow-ing in sin and doubt-ing, Seed for e-ter-ni-ty,
Are you a care-less i-dler? What is your hope and plea?
You shall re-turn re-joic-ing, You shall the Mas-ter see;

Seed from your hand is fall-ing, Oh! what will your har-vest be?
Reap-ing the fruit here-af-ter, Oh! what will your har-vest be?
When you must join the reap-ers, Oh! what will your har-vest be?
When the ripe sheaves are gar-ner'd, Oh! blest will your har-vest be.

What Will Your Harvest Be?—Concluded.

What will your har-vest be, (har-vest be), What will your har - vest be?
Last v. Blest will your har-vest be, (har-vest be,) Blest will your har - vest be.

No. 7.   Oh! 'tis Glory in My Soul.

FLORA L. BEST.   JNO. R. SWENEY.

1. To Thy cross, dear Christ, I'm clinging, All my ref - uge and my plea;
2. Long my heart hath heard Thee call-ing, But I thrust a - side Thy grace;
3. Love e - ter - nal, light e - ter - nal, Close me safe - ly, sweet-ly in;

Match - less is Thy lov - ing-kind-ness, Else it had not stoop'd to me.
Yet, O bound-less con - de - scen-sion, Love is shin - ing from Thy face.
Sav - ior, let Thy balm of heal - ing, Ev - er keep me free from sin.

CHORUS.

Oh, 'tis glo - ry! oh, 'tis glo - ry! Oh, 'tis glo - ry in my soul,

For I've touch'd the hem of His gar - ment, And His pow'r doth make me whole.

By permission.

No. 8. To Save a Poor Sinner Like Me.

Rev. John O. Foster, A. M.   Grace I. Foster.

1. I'll sing of the sto-ry, how Je-sus from glo-ry Has
2. His glo-ry im-mor-tal bright o-ver the por-tal, Has
3. Tho' sea-sons of er-ror and mo-ments of ter-ror, Like
4. My peace like a riv-er flows on-ward for-ev-er, A

saved a poor sin-ner like me; That all who be-lieve Him, and
ban-ished the gloom from the grave; The Lord has as-cend-ed, the
bil-lows of sor-row may roll; In Christ I'm con-fid-ing, In
tide to e-ter-ni-ty's sea, To swell the old sto-ry with

all who re-ceive Him, His bless-ed sal-va-tion may see.
dark-ness is end-ed And now He is might-y to save.
Him I am hid-ing, With safe-ty and rest to my soul.
voi-ces in glo-ry, He saved a poor sin-ner like me.

Chorus.

Then sing the glad cho-rus, His ban-ner is o'er us, His

mer-cy is bound-less and free, From heav-en de-scend-ed, His

By Permission.

To Save a poor Sinner.—Concluded.

love is ex-tend-ed, To save a poor sin-ner like me.

No. 9. Come, Thou Almighty King!

C. WESLEY.   ITALIAN HYMN. 6s, 4s.   FELICE GIARDINI.

1. Come, Thou al-might-y King, Help us Thy name to sing,
2. Come, Thou in-car-nate Word, Gird on Thy might-y sword;
3. Come, ho-ly Com-fort-er! Thy sa-cred wit-ness bear,

Help us to praise; Fa-ther! all-glo-ri-ous, O'er all vic-
Our pray'r at-tend; Come, and Thy peo-ple bless, And give Thy
In this glad hour; Thou, who al-might-y art, Now rule in

to-ri-ous, Come, and reign o-ver us, An-cient of Days!
word suc-cess; Spir-it of ho-li-ness! On us de-scend.
ev-'ry heart, And ne'er from us de-part, Spir-it of pow'r!

No. 10. Drink and Live.

"I Am the Living Water, Drink of Me and ye shall never thirst."—John iv. 14, vi. 35.

P. B.   P. BILHORN.

1. Liv - ing wa - ter pure and free, God hath sent to you and me;
2. Thirst-y souls with care op-press'd, Drink and Christ shall give you rest;
3. Come and drink while 'tis to-day, Come and drink with-out de - lay;

Of the wa - ter Je - sus gives, He who drinks for - ev - er lives.
Why with thirst should sin - ners die, Since life's fount-ain is so nigh.
Come, for this is Je - sus' call, To the fount-ain free to all.

CHORUS.
Come drink of the wa - ter,

Come, drink, drink of the wa - ter, Come drink of the wa - ter of life,

Come drink of the wa - ter, Rit. . . .

Come drink, drink of the wa - ter, While now it is flow-ing for thee, for thee.

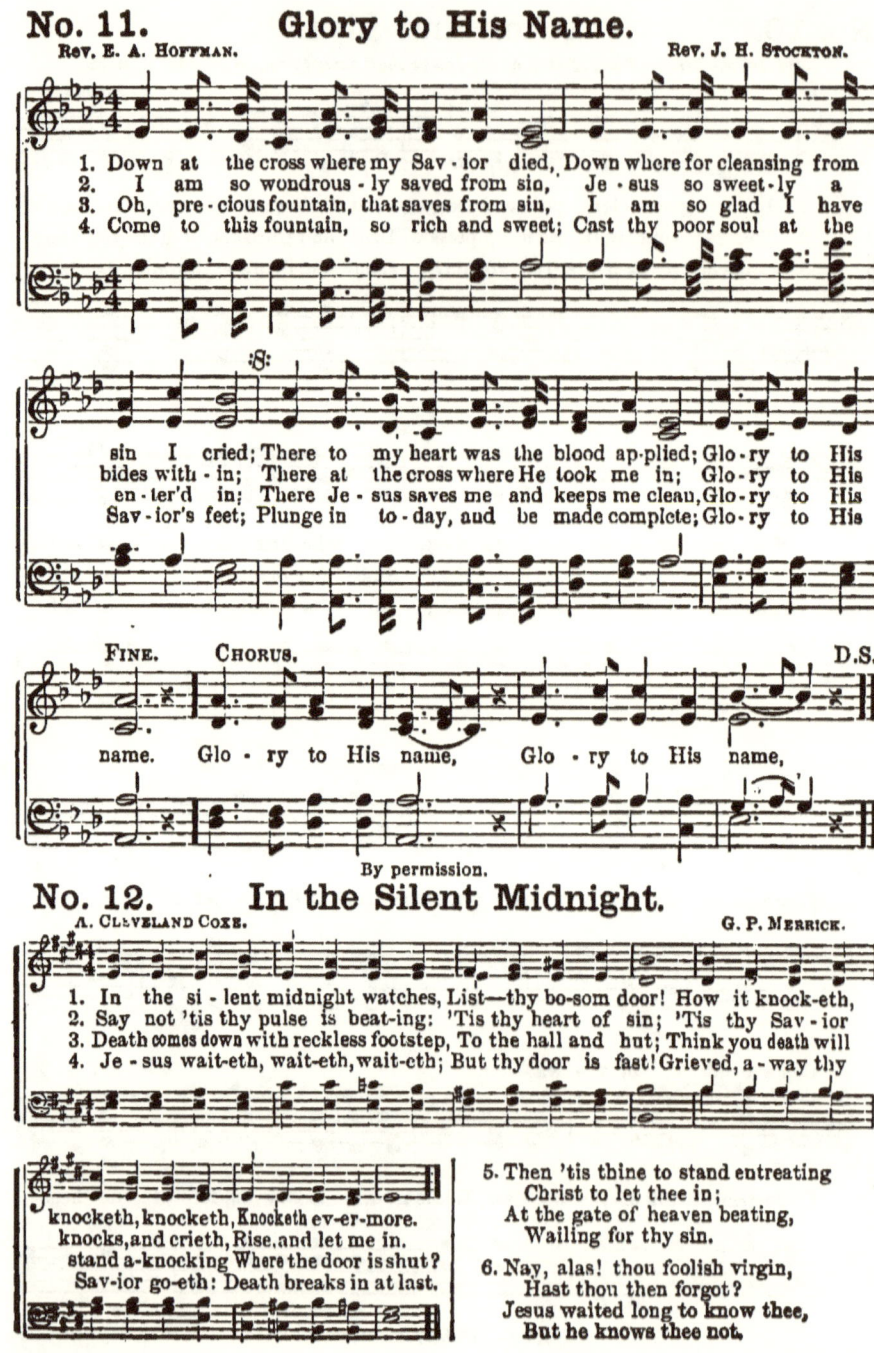

No. 11. Glory to His Name.

Rev. E. A. Hoffman. Rev. J. H. Stockton.

1. Down at the cross where my Sav-ior died, Down where for cleansing from
2. I am so wondrous-ly saved from sin, Je-sus so sweet-ly a
3. Oh, pre-cious fountain, that saves from sin, I am so glad I have
4. Come to this fountain, so rich and sweet; Cast thy poor soul at the

sin I cried; There to my heart was the blood ap-plied; Glo-ry to His
bides with-in; There at the cross where He took me in; Glo-ry to His
en-ter'd in; There Je-sus saves me and keeps me clean, Glo-ry to His
Sav-ior's feet; Plunge in to-day, and be made complete; Glo-ry to His

FINE.   CHORUS.   D.S.

name. Glo-ry to His name, Glo-ry to His name,

By permission.

No. 12. In the Silent Midnight.

A. Cleveland Coxe. G. P. Merrick.

1. In the si-lent midnight watches, List—thy bo-som door! How it knock-eth,
2. Say not 'tis thy pulse is beat-ing: 'Tis thy heart of sin; 'Tis thy Sav-ior
3. Death comes down with reckless footstep, To the hall and hut; Think you death will
4. Je-sus wait-eth, wait-eth, wait-eth; But thy door is fast! Grieved, a-way thy

knocketh, knocketh, Knocketh ev-er-more.
knocks, and crieth, Rise, and let me in.
stand a-knocking Where the door is shut?
Sav-ior go-eth: Death breaks in at last.

5. Then 'tis thine to stand entreating
  Christ to let thee in;
At the gate of heaven beating,
  Wailing for thy sin.

6. Nay, alas! thou foolish virgin,
  Hast thou then forgot?
Jesus waited long to know thee,
  But he knows thee not.

More Like Thee.

W. J. K.

W. J. KIRKPATRICK.

1. Je - sus, Sav - ior, great Ex - am - ple, Pat - tern of all pu - ri - ty,
2. Lest I wan - der from Thy path-way, Or my feet move wear - i - ly,
3. When temp-ta - tions fierce-ly low - er, And my shrinking soul would flee,
4. When a - round me all is dark-ness, And Thy beau-ties none may see,
5. When death's cold, re - pul - sive fin - ger Leaves its im - press on my brow,

I would fol - low in Thy foot-steps, Dai - ly grow-ing more like Thee.
Sav - ior, take my hand and lead me, Keep me stead-fast: more like Thee.
Change each weak - ness in - to pow-er, Keep me spot-less: more like Thee.
May Thy beams, O Glorious Brightness, In ef - ful-gence shine thro' me.
May Thy life, with - in me swell-ing, Keep me sing-ing then as now.

REFRAIN.

More like Thee, more like Thee, Sav-ior, this my constant pray'r shall be,
More like Thee, more like Thee,

Day by day, wher-e'er I stay, Make me more, and more like Thee.

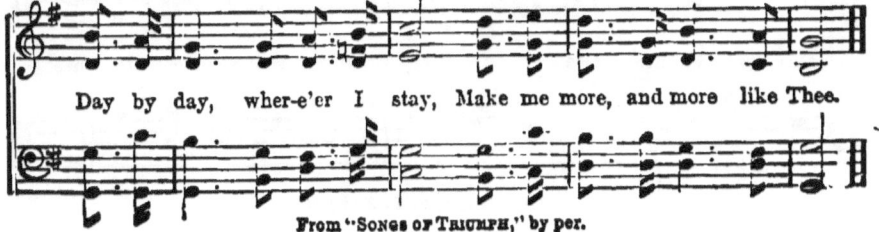

From "Songs of Triumph," by per.

No. 14. Closer to Thee.

The "Lanan"

P. BILHORN.

1. O Je-sus my Lord and my Sav-ior, A rock and a ref-uge to me;
2. Let peace from thy pres-ence pos-sess me, A peace that a-bid-ing shall be;
3. When close by thy side I am keep-ing, My path-way is mark'd out by thee;
4. And when my life's jour-ney is end-ing, The waves of the riv-er I see;

I long to be drawn by thy fa-vor, Still clos-er and clos-er to thee.
And when my temp-ta-tions dis-tress me, O draw me still clos-er to thee.
And rich are the fields for my reap-ing, While clos-er and clos-er to thee.
Let an-gels from glo-ry de-scend-ing, My spir-it bear clos-er to thee.

CHORUS.

Clos-er to thee, clos-er to thee, Clos-er my Lord and my Sav-ior,

Clos-er to thee, clos-er to thee, Draw me still clos-er to thee.

No. 15. Where Will You Stand?

"He shall separate them one from another."—Matt. xxv. 32.

P. B.

P. Bilhorn.

1. Oh, broth - er, which side of the Lord will you stand, In the
2. The day of the Lord is most cer - tain to come, And in
3. The ref - uge of lies will be then swept a - way, The

day when the judg-ment has come, When the Lord shall come forth, with the
judg - ment we all must ap - pear, Where Christ will be judge of the
se - crets of hearts be made known, The Mas - ter will say to the

book in His hand, To reck - on with ev - 'ry one.
quick and the dead, Oh, broth - er, you too will be there.
faith - ful, well done, To the wick - ed, de - part and be gone.

CHORUS.

Oh, where will you stand, Oh,
Oh, where, oh, where will you stand, will you stand, Oh,

Where Will You Stand?—Concluded.

where   will you stand, you stand, When the Lord shall come forth,
where, oh, where will you stand, you stand,

With the book in His hand, To reck - on with ev - 'ry one.

No. 16. Come, Sinners, Come!

P. BILHORN.   A. BEIRLY.

1. Come, sin-ners, come to Je - sus now, While mer-cy stands entreating;
   The Spir - it and the Bride say come, The Sav-ior's voice is (*omit*) plead-ing.

2. Come, wea - ry one, dis-tress'd with sin, His blood still is the to-ken;
   A full a - tone-ment He hath made, The way to life is (*omit*) o-pen.

D. C. *The rich, the poor, the lost, the blind, Come, ev-'ry tribe and (omit) na-tion.*

Come, sin - ners, come, be - fore Him bow, And find in Him sal - va - tion;

3 Come, burden'd heart, and all oppress'd,
  Come, Jesus has forgiven;
  He is the life, the truth, the rest,
  The only way to heaven.

4 I come, O Lord, I come to-day,
  Forsaking sinful pleasure;
  O do not turn from me away,
  But be my only treasure.

The Prodigal Child.

E. C. A.

E. C. Avis.

Not too fast.

1. O, prod-i-gal, come, I am wait-ing, Why tar-ry on mountains so bare?
2. O, prod-i-gal, come, I am wait-ing, The Sav-ior said sweetly and low;
3. O, prod-i-gal, come, I am wait-ing, From pleasures of sin turn a-way;
4. O, prod-i-gal, come, I am wait-ing, E-ter-ni-ty now draweth nigh;

Why per-ish with cold and with hun-ger? There's bread enough yet and to spare.
Thy sins tho' they be red as scar-let, I'll make them as white as the snow.
Make haste and come back to thy Fa-ther, Thy soul may be lost in de-lay!
Re-turn and be-lieve on the Sav-ior, And thou shalt have treasures on high.

REFRAIN.

come home,........

Come home, Come home, O prod-i-gal child, come home, O come home,

Come home, Come home,

And squander thy substance no long-er; O prod-i-gal child, come home.

No. 18. The Savior is My All in All.

"Wherefore He is able to save them to the uttermost."—Heb. vii: 25.

P. B.   P. Bilhorn.

1. The Sav-iour is my all in all, He is my con-stant theme!
2. His Spir-it gives sweet peace with-in, And bids all care de-part!
3. And what-so-ev-er I may ask, To glo-ri-fy His Name,
4. Oh, praise the Lord, my soul, re-joice, Give thanks un-to thy God!

By sim-ply trust-ing in His word, He keeps me pure and clean.
He fills my soul with right-eous-ness, And pu-ri-fies the heart.
The Fa-ther free-ly gives to me, Since Christ the Sav-iour came.
Who took thee in thy sin-ful-ness, And cleansed thee by His blood!

Chorus.

Glo-ry! oh, glo-ry! Je-sus hath re-deemed me;

rit.

Glo-ry! oh, glo-ry! He washed my sins a-way, a-way!

No. 19. I will Sing the Wondrous Story.

"I will sing of the mercies of the Lord forever.—"Ps. 1: 89.

F. H. Rowley.   Peter Bilhorn.

1. I will sing the won-drous sto - ry, Of the Christ who died for me,
2. I was lost, but Je - sus found me, Found the sheep that went a - stray;
3. I was bruised, but Je - sus healed me, Faint was I from many a fall,
4. Days of dark - ness still come o'er me, Sor - row's paths I oft - en tread,
5. He will keep me till the riv - er Rolls its wa - ters at my feet;

How He left His home in glo - ry, For the cross on Cal - va - ry.
Threw His lov - ing arms a - round me, Drew me back in - to His way.
Sight was gone, and fears possessed me, But He freed me from them all.
But the Sav - ior still is with me, By His hand I'm safe - ly led.
Then He'll bear me safe - ly o - ver, Where the loved ones I shall meet.

Chorus.

Yes I'll sing.......... the won - drous sto - - - - ry
Yes, I'll sing   *the won-drous sto - ry*

Of the Christ......... who died for me,...............
of the Christ   *who died for me,*

Sing it with......... the saints in glo - - - ry,
Sing it with   *the saints in glo - ry,*

I will Sing.—Concluded.

Gath - ered by............ the crys - tal sea.
Gath - ered by the crys - tal sea, the crys - tal sea.

No. 20. Savior, Pilot Me.

J. E. GOULD.

1. Je - sus, Sa - vior, pi - lot me O - ver life's tem-pest - uous sea;
2. When th' A - pos - tles' fra - gile bark Strug-gled with the bil - lows dark,
3. As a moth - er stills her child Thou canst hush the o - cean wild;
4. When at last I near the shore, And the fear - ful break-ers roar

Un - known waves be - fore me roll, Hid - ing rock and treacherous shoal;
On the storm - y Gal - i - lee, Thou did'st walk a - cross the sea;
Bois-terous waves o - bey Thy will When Thou say'st to them "Be still."
'Twixt me and the peace - ful rest. Then, while lean - ing on Thy breast,

Chart and com - pass came from Thee: Je - sus, Sav - ior, pi - lot me.
And when they be - held Thy form, Safe they glid - ed thro' the storm.
Won - drous Sov - ereign of the sea, Je - sus, Sav - ior, pi - lot me.
May I hear Thee say to me, "Fear not I will pi - lot thee."

Beulah Land.

EDGAR PAGE.

JNO. R. SWENEY, by per.

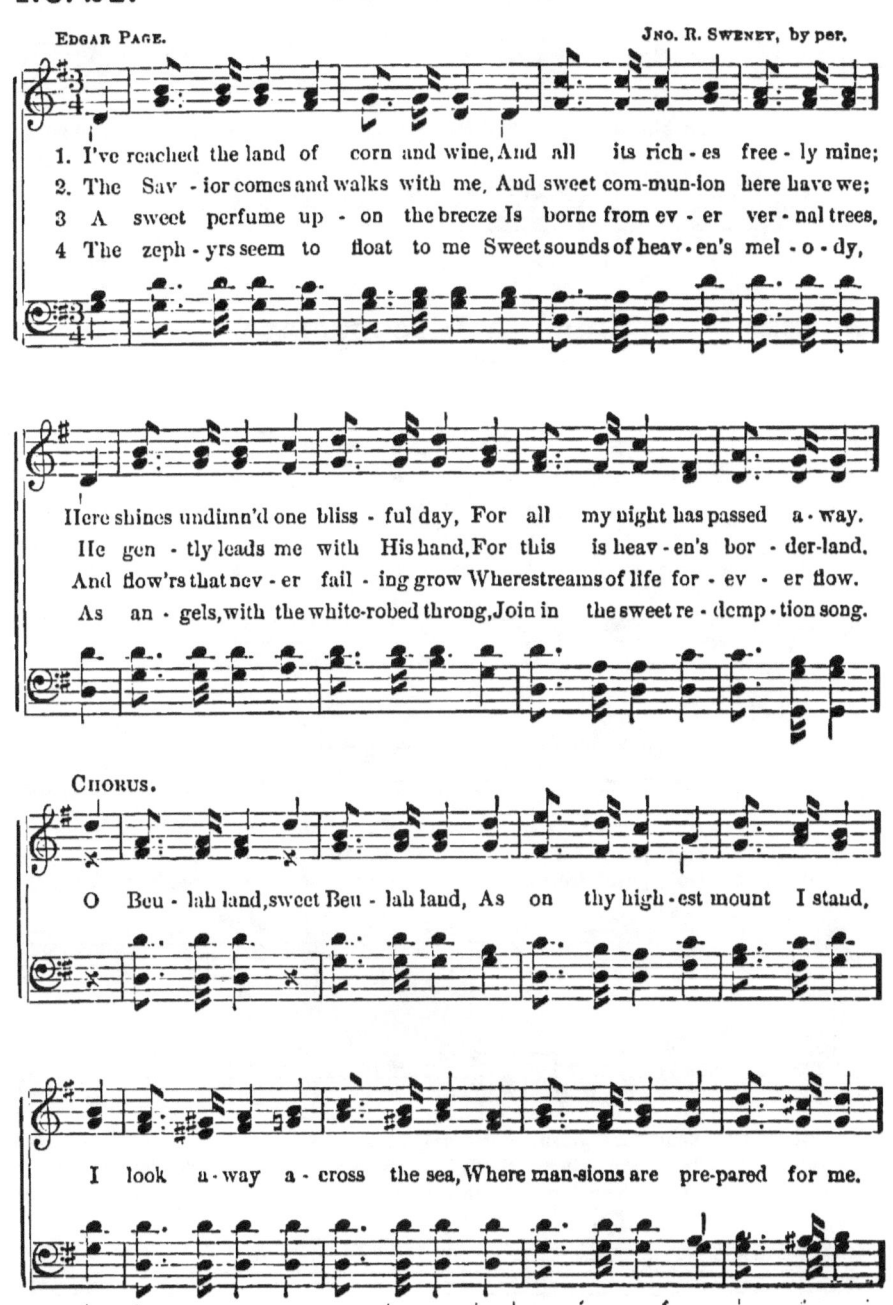

1. I've reached the land of corn and wine, And all its rich-es free-ly mine;
2. The Sav-ior comes and walks with me, And sweet com-mun-ion here have we;
3. A sweet perfume up-on the breeze Is borne from ev-er ver-nal trees,
4. The zeph-yrs seem to float to me Sweet sounds of heav-en's mel-o-dy,

Here shines undimm'd one bliss-ful day, For all my night has passed a-way.
He gen-tly leads me with His hand, For this is heav-en's bor-der-land.
And flow'rs that nev-er fail-ing grow Where streams of life for-ev-er flow.
As an-gels, with the white-robed throng, Join in the sweet re-demp-tion song.

CHORUS.

O Beu-lah land, sweet Beu-lah land, As on thy high-est mount I stand,

I look a-way a-cross the sea, Where man-sions are pre-pared for me.

Beulah Land.—Concluded.

And view the shin-ing glo-ry shore, My heav'n, my home for-ev-er-more.

No. 22.   Come, ye Disconsolate.

THOS. MOORE.   SAMUEL WEBBE.

1. Come, ye dis-con-so-late! wher-e'er ye lan-guish, Come to the
2. Joy of the des-o-late! light of the stray-ing, Hope of the
3. Here see the bread of life: see wa-ters flow-ing, Forth from the

mer-cy-seat, fer-vent-ly kneel: Here bring your wound-ed hearts,
pen-i-tent, fade-less and pure! Here speaks the Com-fort-er,
throne of God, pure from a-bove: Come to the feast of love;

here tell your an-guish; Earth has no sor-row that heav'n can-not heal.
ten-der-ly say-ing, Earth has no sor-row that heav'n can-not cure.
come, ev-er know-ing, Earth has no sor-rows but heav'n can re-move.

No. 23. Sweet Peace the Gift of God's Love.

P. B.

P. BILHORN.

1. There comes to my heart one sweet strain, (sweet strain,) A
2. By Christ on the cross peace was made, (was made,) My
3. When Je- sus as Lord I had crowned, (had crowned,) My
4. In Je- sus for peace I a- bide, (a- bide,) And

glad and a joy- ous re- frain, (re- frain,) I
debt by his death was all paid, (all paid,) No
heart with this peace did a- bound, (a- bound,) In
as I keep close to His side, (His side,) There's

sing it a-gain and a- gain, Sweet peace, the gift of God's love.
oth- er foun-da-tion is laid For peace, the gift of God's love.
Him the rich bless-ing I found, Sweet peace, the gift of God's love.
noth- ing but peace doth be- tide, Sweet peace, the gift of God's love.

CHORUS.

Peace, peace, sweet peace, Won- der-ful gift from a- bove, (a- bove,)

Sweet Peace.—Concluded.

Rit.

Oh, won-der-ful, won-der-ful peace, Sweet peace, the gift of God's love.

No. 24. He Knows.

P. BILHORN.

1. He knows the bit - ter, wea - ry way, The
2. He knows when faint and worn we sink, How
3. He knows! oh, thought so full of bliss! For
4. He knows! oh, heart, take up thy cross, And

end - less striv - ing, day by day, The souls that weep, the
deep the pain, how near the brink Of dark de - spair, we
though on earth our joy we miss, We still can bear it
know earth's treas - ures are but dross, And all will prove as

souls that pray, He knows! He knows! He knows!
pause and shrink, He knows! He knows! He knows!
feel - ing this, He knows! He knows! He knows!
gain or loss! He knows! He knows! He knows!

Calvary.

" The place which is called Calvary, there they crucified Him."—Luke xxiii. 33.

Rev. W. M'K. Darwood. Jno. R. Sweney.

1. On Cal-v'ry's brow my Sav-ior died, 'Twas there my
   On Calv'ry's brow my Sav-ior died,
2. 'Mid rend-ing rocks and dark'ning skies, My Sav-ior
   'Mid rending rocks and dark'ning skies,
3. O Je-sus, Lord, how can it be, That Thou should'st
   O Je-sus, Lord, how can it be,

Lord was cru-ci-fied; 'Twas on the cross he bled for
'Twas there my Lord, was cru-ci-fied, 'Twas on the cross
bows His head and dies; The op'ning veil re-veals the
My Sav-ior bows His head and dies; The op'ning veil
give Thy life for me, To bear the cross and ag-o-
That Thou should'st give Thy life for me, To bear the cross

me, And purchased there my par-don free.
he bled for me, And purchased there
way To heav-en's joys and end-less day.
re-veals the way To heav-en's joys
ny, In that dread hour on Cal-va-ry!—
and ag-o-ny, In that dread hour

REFRAIN.

O Cal-va-ry! dark Cal-va-ry! Where Je-sus shed His blood for me, for me;

By permission.

Calvary—Concluded.

O Cal - va - ry! blest Cal - va - ry! 'Twas there my Sav - ior died for me.

No. 26.   It Reaches Me.

MARY D. JAMES.   JNO. R. SWENEY.

1. Oh, this ut - ter-most sal - va - tion! 'Tis a fount - ain full and free,
2. How a - maz - ing God's com - pas-sion, That so vile a worm should prove
3. Je - sus, Sav - ior, I a - dore Thee! Now Thy love I will pro - claim,

Pure, ex - haust - less, ev - er flow-ing, Won-drous grace! it reach-es me!
This stu - pen - dous bliss of Heav - en, This un - measured wealth of love!
I will tell the bless-ed sto - ry, I will mag - ni - fy Thy name!

CHORUS.

It reach-es me! it reach-es me! Won-drous grace! it reach-es me!

Pure, ex - haust - less, ev - er flow-ing, Wondrous grace! it reach - es me!

By permission.

No. 27. Soon Will The Mist Roll Away.

GEO. COOPER.

H. M.

1. Yon-der's the land where the lov'd ones are, Soon will the mist roll a-way!
2. Dark looms the path, but the promise heed, Soon will the mist roll a-way!
3. Bear thou the Cross till the Crown is won, Soon will the mist roll a-way!

Joy soon to rest in that realm a far, Soon will the mist roll a-way!
Je-sus a-lone can re-lieve thy need, Soon will the mist roll a-way!
Work till the will of the Lord be done, Soon will the mist roll a-way!

There in the loving smile of Je-sus to bide, Vis-ions of glo-ry day by day!
Clear will the purpose of the Lord be to thee, Has-ten the Master to o-bey;
All will be re-conciled to thee by and by, Faith guideth on to per fect day;

Faith fondly whispers, while in shadows we hide, Soon will the mist roll a-way!
Bliss-ful the vis-ion that beyond we shall see, Soon will the mist roll a-way!
Soon shall the glo-ry dawn up-on ev-ery eye, Soon will the mist roll a-way!

Yon-der's the land where the lov'd ones are, Soon will the mist roll a-way!

By permission.

Soon Will the Mist.—Concluded.

Joy soon to rest in that realm a-far, Soon will the mist roll a-way!

No. 28. ### Stand up for Jesus.

G. DUFFIELD.

G. J. WEBBE.

1. Stand up!—stand up for Je-sus! Ye sol-diers of the cross;

Lift high the roy-al ban-ner, It must not suf-fer loss:

Fine.

D. S. Till ev-'ry foe is van-quished, And Christ is Lord in-deed.

D.S.

From vic-t'ry un-to vic-t'ry His arm-y shall he lead.

2 Stand up!—stand up for Jesus!
   Stand in His strength alone,
The arm of flesh will fail you—
   Ye dare not trust your own:
Put on the gospel armor,
   And, watching unto prayer,
Where duty calls or danger,
   Be never wanting there.

3 Stand up!—stand up for Jesus!
   The strife will not be long;
This day the noise of battle,
   The next, the victor's song:
To him that overcometh,
   A crown of life shall be;
He with the King of glory
   Shall reign eternally!

No. 29. The City of Gold.

P. BILHORN.

F. C. AVIS.

1. There's a prom - ise re-cord - ed in God's ho - ly word, It is
2. In this world we have sor - rows and troub - les and cares, But we'll
3. There all sick - ness and sor - row and death are unknown; There the

bless - ed in beau - ty un - told; That we nev - er shall hun - ger, or
en - ter with Je - sus the fold; He will lead us a - long thro' the
glo - ries on glo - ries un - fold; There the Lamb is the light in the

thirst an - y more, In that won - der - ful cit - y of gold.
pas - tures so green, In that won - der - ful cit - y of gold.
midst of the throne, In that won - der - ful cit - y of gold.

CHORUS.

There we'll dwell ev - er-more, And we'll nev - - - er grow old;
There we'll dwell ev - er-more, And we'll nev - er grow old;

By permission.

The City of Gold—Concluded.

There the righteous for-ev-er Shall shine like the stars, In that wonderful cit-y of gold.

No. 30.

MRS. M. E. GATES.
With Expression.

Thy Love to Me.

(Jer. xxxi. 3.)

E. C AVIS.

1. Thy love to me, O Christ, Thy love to me, Not mine to Thee, I plead,
2. Thy rec-ord I be-lieve, Thy word to me; Thy love I now re-ceive,
3. Im - mor-tal love of Thine, Thy sac-ri-fice, In - fi-nite need of mine,
4. Let me more clear-ly trace Thy love to me, See in the Fa-ther's face

Not mine to Thee! This is my com-fort strong, This is my
Full, change-less, free: Love from the sin-less Son, Love to the
On - ly sup-plies, Streams of di-vin-est pow'r Flow to me,
His love for thee; Know as He loves the Son, So dost thou

on - ly song, Thy love, O Christ, to me, Thy love to me.
sin - ful one, Thy love, O Christ, to me, Thy love to me.
ev - 'ry hour, Thy love, O Christ, to me, Thy love to me.
love thine own: Thy love, O Christ, to me, Thy love to me.

No. 31. Precious the Blood.

P. H. ROBLIN.　　　　　　　　　　　　　　　　　P. BILHORN.

1. The Sav - ior shed His pre - cious blood On Calvary's rug - ged tree,
2. That pre - cious blood be - fore the throne, Speaks par - don full and free,
3. The pre - cious blood, the pre - cious blood, O pre - cious let it be,

Poor sin - ners lost to bring to God, 'Twas all for you and me.
For all who will the Sav - ior own, It pleads for you and me.
Con - fess the name of Christ thy Lord, And from thy sin be free.

CHORUS.

Pre - cious the blood, . . It cleans - eth us white, . .

Precious the blood it cleanseth us white, Cleanseth us whiter, yes, whiter than snow;

Pre - cious the blood, . . It cleanseth us whiter than snow. . .

Precious the blood of the Lamb that was Slain, It cleanseth us whiter, yes, whiter than snow.

Pre - cious the blood, . It cleanseth us whiter than snow. .

Nearer the Cross.

Mrs. F. J. Crosby.

Mrs. J. F. Knapp, by per.

1. "Near-er the cross!" my heart can say, I am com-ing near-er, Near-er the cross from day to day, I am com-ing near-er; Near-er the cross where Je-sus died, Near-er the foun-tain's crim-son tide, Near-er my Sav-ior's wound-ed side, I am com-ing near-er, I am com-ing near-er.

2. Near-er the Christian's mer-cy seat, I am com-ing near-er, Feast-ing my soul on man-na sweet, I am com-ing near-er; Stron-ger in faith, more clear I see Je-sus who gave Him-self for me; Near-er to Him I still would be: Still I'm com-ing near-er, Still I'm com-ing near-er.

3. Near-er in pray'r my hope as-pires, I am com-ing near-er, Deep-er the love my soul desires, I am com-ing near-er; Near-er the end of toil and care, Near-er the joy I long to share, Near-er the crown I soon shall wear: I am com-ing near-er, I am com-ing near-er.

No. 33.

Life Evermore.

John iii. 7.

E. W. OAKES.

P. BILHORN.

1. Oh, let the words of Je-sus ring From east to west, from shore to shore;
2. No works of thine can give the right To en-ter heav-en's o-pen door;
3. 'Tis all of grace, a-bun-dant grace, His word de-clares it o'er and o'er,
4. He's read-y now to cleanse thy heart, If you His Spir-it's pow'r im-plore;

You must, you must be born a-gain, To live for ev-er-more.
Christ is the Way, the Truth, the Light, And Life for ev-er-more.
Who-e'er be-lieves on Je-sus Christ Shall live for ev-er-more.
The gift of life He will im-part, Yea, life for ev-er-more.

CHORUS.

You must be born a-gain, a-gain, You must be born a-gain, a-gain;

To live with Christ for ev-er-more, You must be born a-gain.

No. 34. The Book of Life.

W. A. O.

W. A. OGDEN.

1. In the Lamb's Book of Life Will my name there ap-pear? Shall I
2. Un-to me a new name In His king-dom He'll give; Of the
3. There shall noth-ing be hid From the eyes of His own, When in

walk in white rai-ment? Will Je-sus be near? With the dear ones of
man-na that's hid-den From Him I'll re-ceive; And my name He'll con-
glo-ry we view Him Up-on the great throne; Then to Him shall a-

earth Who have pass'd on be-fore, Shall I dwell in that coun-try And
fess To the Fa-ther a-bove; Oh, then, bless-ed be God for The
rise From the saved a-mong men, Un-to Him be the glo-ry For-

CHORUS.

sor-row no more? Glo-ry to God! His prom-ise is
Son of His love. Glo-ry, etc.
ev-er, A-men. Glo-ry, etc.

dear; I re-joice, for I know that my name's writ-ten there.

By permission.

The New Song.

No. 35. Flora L. Best.   Jno. R. Sweney.

Moderato.

1. There are songs of joy that I loved to sing, When my heart was as blithe as a
2. Can my lips be mute, or my heart be sad, When the gra-cious Mas-ter hath
3. I shall catch the gleam of its jas-per wall, When I come to the gloom of the

bird in spring; But the song I have learn'd is so full of cheer, That the
made me glad? When He points where the man-y bright mansions be, And
e-ven fall, For I know that the shad-ows so dreary and dim, Have a

dawn shines out in the darkness drear. O, the new, new song, O, the
sweet-ly says, "There is one for thee?" O, the new, new song,
path of light that will lead to Him.

new, new song, I can sing it now With the
O, the new, new song, I can sing just now

ran - som'd throng: Pow-er and do-min-ion to Him that shall
ransom'd, the ransom'd throng:

CHORUS. *A little faster*

By Permission.

The New Song.—Concluded.

reign,
that shall reign,

Glo - ry and praise to the Lamb that was slain.

Oh, Happy Day.

E. F. RIMBAULT.

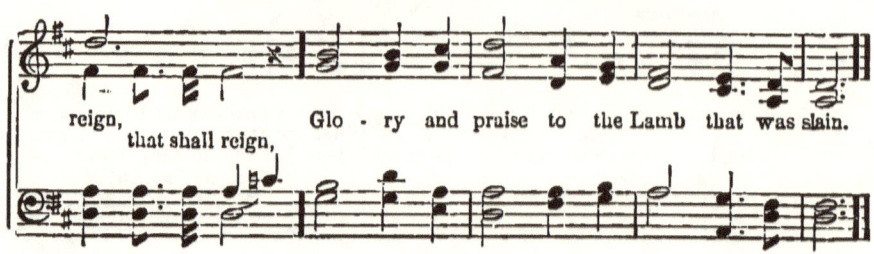

1. Oh, hap - py day, that fixed my choice, On Thee my Sav - iour, and my God!
Well may this glow - ing heart re - joice, And tell its rapt - ures all a - broad.

S. CHORUS.

FINE.

Hap - py day, hap - py day, When Je - sus washed my sins a - way,

D.S.

He taught me how to watch and pray, And live re - joic - ing ev - 'ry day.

2 'Tis done, the great transaction's done;
I am the Lord's and He is mine;
He drew me and I follow'd on,
Charmed to confess the voice divine.

3 Now rest, my long-divided heart!
Fixed on this blissful center, rest;
Nor ever from thy Lord depart,
With Him, of every good possessed.

No. 37. Conquer Through His Word.

Miss J. H. JOHNSTON.   P. BILHORN.

1. I've en-list-ed in the ar-my of the Lord, He has armed me
2. 'Tis an ar-my that is ev-er sure to win! 'Tis the Lord who
3. There are foes on ev-ery hand, who seek to harm, But with us there
4. Come and join this conqu'ring ar-my of the Lord; Let Him give to

with a hel-met, shield and sword, Now to bat-tle for the right, by the
leads a-gainst the host of sin; Thro' the word that giv-eth light, we shall
is an ev-er-last-ing arm; With our Cap-tain in command, we are
you a hel-met, shield and sword; By the power of Je-sus' might, you may

power of Je-sus' might, By His grace I'll con-quer thro' His word.
con-quer in the fight, Tho' the en-e-my be strong with-in.
strong in heart and hand, And se-cure a-gainst all false a-larm.
bat-tle for the right, You may tri-umph thro' His roy-al word.

CHORUS.

Hal-le-lu-jah! Hal-le-lu-jah! Prais-es
Hal-le-lu-jah! Hal-le-lu-jah!

Conquer Through His.—Concluded.

to His ev - er - last - ing name we'll sing, Hal - le - lu - jah!

Hal - le - lu - jah!

Hal le lu - jah! We shall con - quer thro' our Lord and King.

Hal - le - lu - jah!

No. 38.

Heaven is my Home.

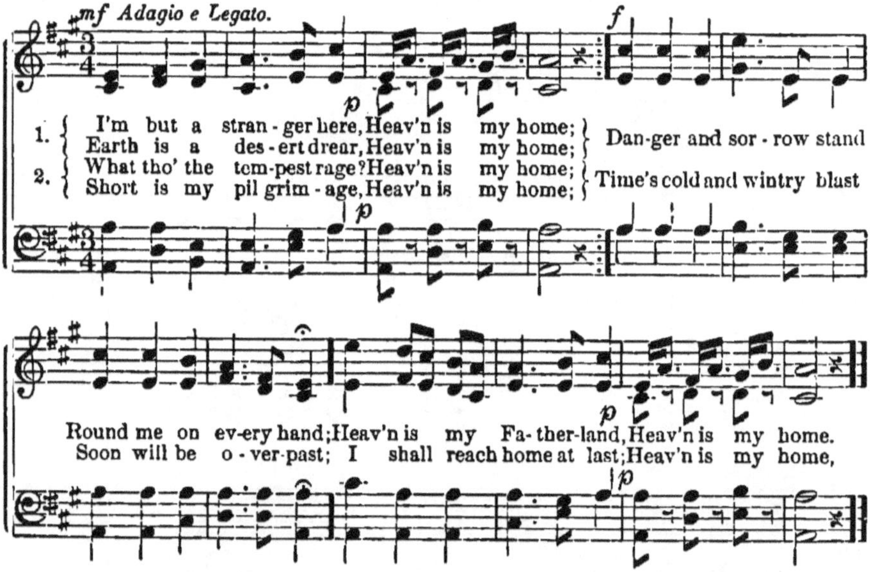

mf Adagio e Legato.

p *f*

1. { I'm but a stran - ger here, Heav'n is my home; }
   { Earth is a des - ert drear, Heav'n is my home; } Dan - ger and sor - row stand

2. { What tho' the tem - pest rage? Heav'n is my home; }
   { Short is my pil grim - age, Heav'n is my home; } Time's cold and wintry blast

p

Round me on ev-ery hand; Heav'n is my Fa - ther-land, Heav'n is my home.

Soon will be o - ver-past; I shall reach home at last; Heav'n is my home,

p

3 Peace! O my troubled soul,
　Heav'n is my home;
I soon shall reach the goal;
　Heav'n is my home;
Swiftly the race I'll run,
Yield up my crown to none;
Forward! the prize is won;
　Heav'n is my home.

4 There, at my Savior's side,
　Heav'n is my home;
I shall be glorified;
　Heav'n is my home;
There are the good and blest,
Those I loved most and best,
There, too, I soon shall rest.
　Heav'n is my home.

No. 39. I Am Coming, Lord, to Thee.

W. A. O.   *"In returning, ye shall be saved."*—Isa. xxx. 15.   W. A. OGDEN.

Earnestly

1. I am com-ing, Lord, to Thee, with a trem-bling heart, I am
2. I am com-ing, Lord, to Thee, with my load of sin, I am
3. I am com-ing, Lord, to Thee, but my faith is weak, I am

com-ing with my soul dis-trest, To Thy prom-ise now I fly,
com-ing, wea-ry, faint, and sore, Tho' I've slight-ed oft Thy grace,
com-ing, wilt Thou hear my cry? I have heard Thy gra-cious call,

Leave, oh, leave me not to die, I am com-ing, Lord, to Thee, for rest.
And have turned from Thee my face, I am com-ing, Lord, to roam no more.
At Thy lov-ing feet I fall, I am com-ing, tho' I faint and die.

CHORUS.

Com-ing, Lord, to Thee, Com-ing, Lord, to Thee,

I am com-ing,.... I am

Com-ing with my soul dis-trest, Com-ing, Lord, to Thee,

By permission.

I am Coming, Lord—Concluded.

com - ing, ...

com - ing, Lord, to Thee, I am com-ing, Lord, to Thee for rest.

No. 40. I am Saved.

Mrs. S. L. OBERHOLTZER.

JNO. R. SWENEY.

1. I am sav'd! the Lord hath sav'd me, Help me shout the glo-rious news!
2. Loud I sing my ex - ul - ta - tion, Hop-ing it will reach the skies,
3. Free sal - va - tion! glad sal - va - tion! Let us shout from pole to pole,
4. When at last the days are gath - er'd In - to Thy great judg-ment one,

I have tast - ed God's sal - va - tion, And 'tis sweet as hon-eyed dews.
Keep, dear Lord, my soul for - ev - er Un - der Thy pro - tect-ing eyes.
Un - til each dis - eas - ed na - tion Feels that God hath made it whole.
May I find my name deep writ-ten In the rec-ords of Thy Son.

CHORUS.

Glo - ry, glo - ry, hal - le - lu - jah! I re - joice sal - va-tion came;

Glo - ry, glo - ry, hal - le - lu - jah! I am sav'd in Je - sus' name.

No. 41. He is Calling You To-Day.

"To-day if you will hear my voice, harden not your hearts."

P. B.

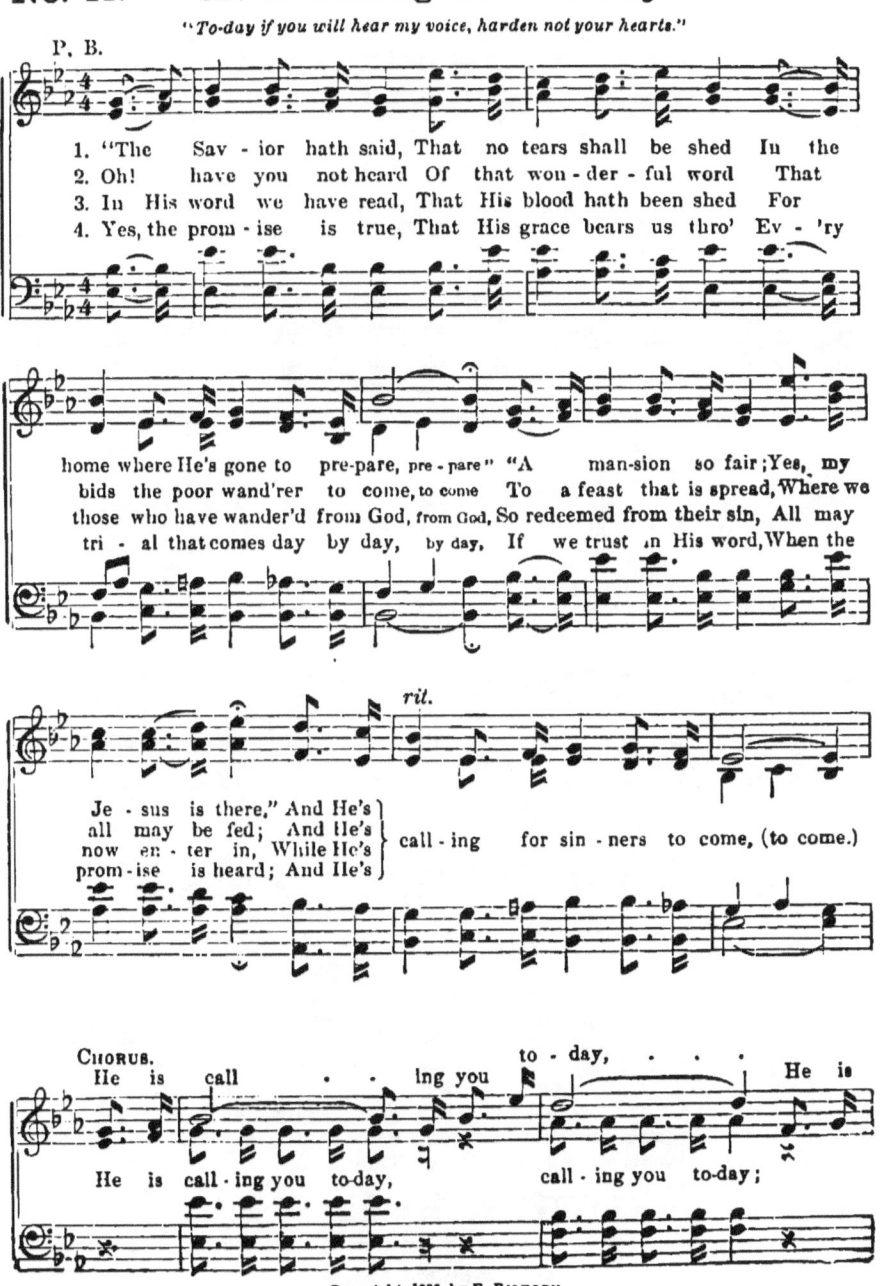

1. "The Sav-ior hath said, That no tears shall be shed In the
2. Oh! have you not heard Of that won-der-ful word That
3. In His word we have read, That His blood hath been shed For
4. Yes, the prom-ise is true, That His grace bears us thro' Ev-'ry

home where He's gone to pre-pare, pre-pare" "A man-sion so fair; Yes, my
bids the poor wand'rer to come, to come To a feast that is spread, Where we
those who have wander'd from God, from God, So redeemed from their sin, All may
tri-al that comes day by day, by day, If we trust in His word, When the

Je-sus is there," And He's }
all may be fed; And He's }
now en-ter in, While He's } call-ing for sin-ners to come, (to come.)
prom-ise is heard; And He's }

CHORUS.

He is call - - ing you to - day, . . . He is
He is call-ing you to-day, call-ing you to-day;

He is Calling You To-Day—Concluded.

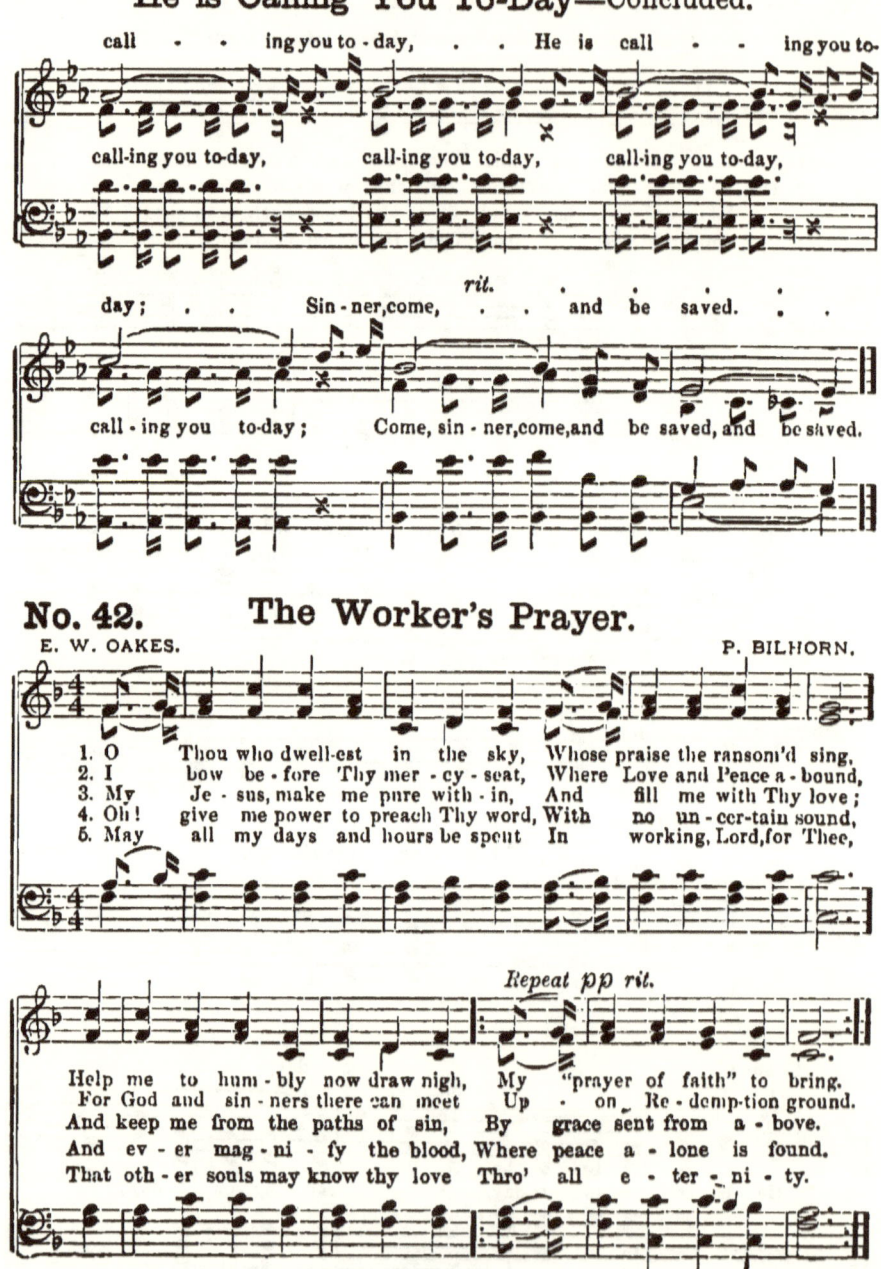

call - - ing you to-day, . . He is call - - ing you to-
call-ing you to-day, call-ing you to-day, call-ing you to-day,

day; . . Sin - ner, come, . . and be saved. . .
call - ing you to-day; Come, sin - ner, come, and be saved, and be saved.

No. 42. The Worker's Prayer.

E. W. OAKES.   P. BILHORN.

1. O   Thou who dwell-est   in the sky,   Whose praise the ransom'd sing,
2. I   bow be - fore Thy mer - cy - seat,   Where Love and Peace a - bound.
3. My   Je - sus, make me pure with - in,   And   fill me with Thy love;
4. Oh! give me power to preach Thy word, With   no un - cer-tain sound,
5. May all my days and hours be spent In   working, Lord, for Thee,

Repeat pp rit.

Help me to hum - bly now draw nigh, My "prayer of faith" to bring.
For God and sin - ners there can meet Up - on Re - demp-tion ground.
And keep me from the paths of sin, By   grace sent from a - bove.
And ev - er mag - ni - fy the blood, Where peace a - lone is found.
That oth - er souls may know thy love Thro' all e - ter - ni - ty.

No.43. We shall See Him and be Like Him.

P. B.   P. BILHORN.

1. Bless-ed be the God and Fa-ther of our Sav-ior Je-sus Christ, Thro' great
2. Think, be-lov - ed, now are we the sons of God by grace di-vine, And it
3. So re-joice with joy un-speak-a - ble and full of glo - ry too, Tho' as

mer - cy He a liv-ing hope has giv'n, Let the ran-som'd join and sing Hal-le-
doth not yet ap-pear what we shall be, When our blessed Lord shall come all His
yet we have not seen our bless-ed Lord; But His Spir-it fills the heart, while the

lu - jah to our King, We shall see Him and be like Him ev - er - more.
ran-som'd to call home, We shall see Him and be like Him ev - er - more.
word doth joy im - part, We shall see Him and be like Him ev - er - more.

CHORUS.

We shall see   Him   and be like   Him,   We shall

We shall see Him and be like Him, We shall see Him and be like Him,

We shall See Him—Concluded.

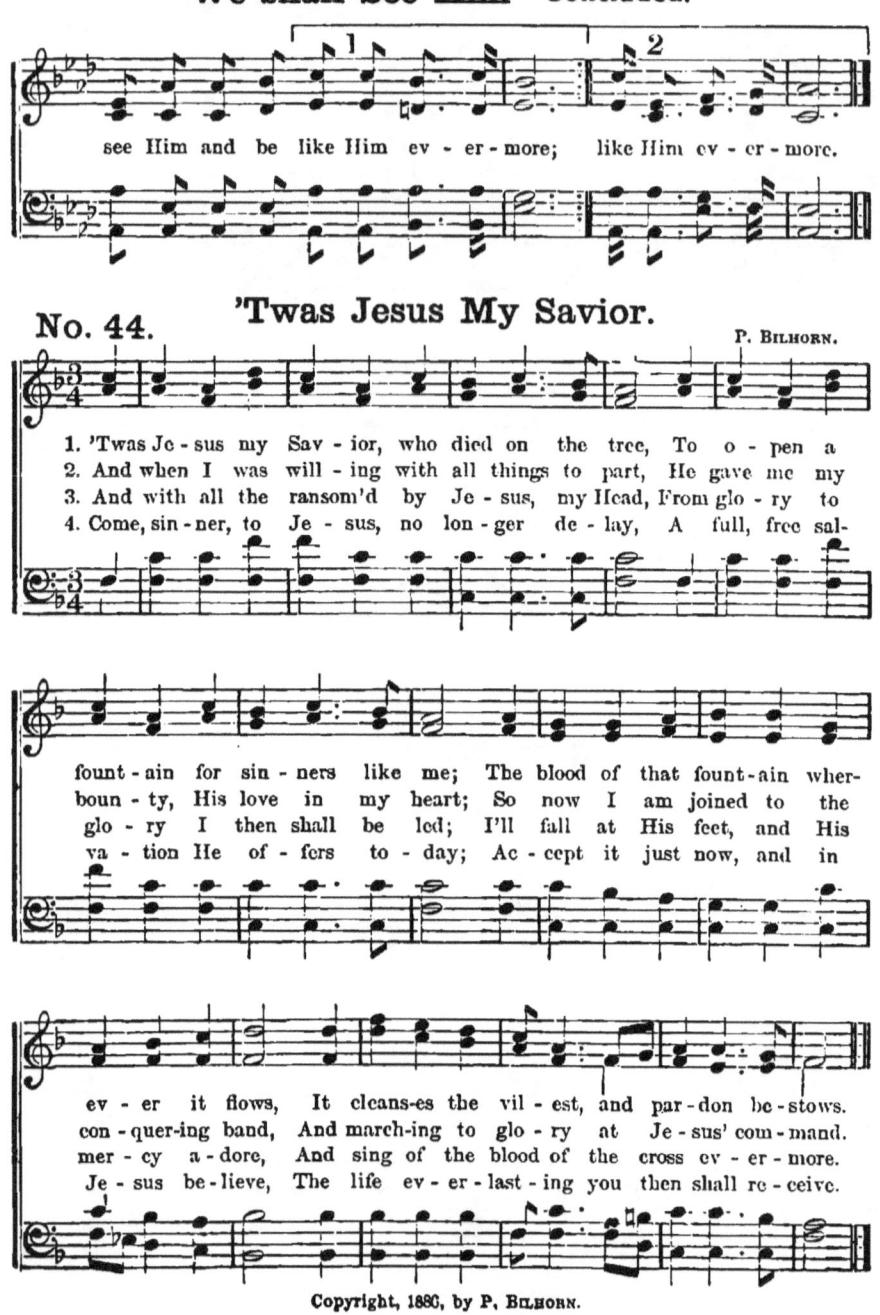

see Him and be like Him ev - er-more; like Him ev - er - more.

No. 44. 'Twas Jesus My Savior.

P. BILHORN.

1. 'Twas Je - sus my Sav - ior, who died on the tree, To o - pen a
2. And when I was will - ing with all things to part, He gave me my
3. And with all the ransom'd by Je - sus, my Head, From glo - ry to
4. Come, sin - ner, to Je - sus, no lon - ger de - lay, A full, free sal -

fount - ain for sin - ners like me; The blood of that fount - ain wher-
boun - ty, His love in my heart; So now I am joined to the
glo - ry I then shall be led; I'll fall at His feet, and His
va - tion He of - fers to - day; Ac - cept it just now, and in

ev - er it flows, It cleans-es the vil - est, and par-don be-stows.
con - quer-ing band, And march-ing to glo - ry at Je - sus' com - mand.
mer - cy a - dore, And sing of the blood of the cross ev - er - more.
Je - sus be - lieve, The life ev - er - last - ing you then shall re - ceive.

No. 45. Jesus All-Sufficient.

JULIA H. JOHNSTON.　　　　　　　　　　　　　ALFRED BEIRLY.

1. Je - sus, ev - er pres-ent Friend, Whom have I on earth be - side?
2. Je - sus, Sav - ior, when a - lone Thou didst bear my load of sin,
3. By thy death my debt was paid, All my life to Thee I owe,
4 Weak and help - less, sure to stray, I am noth-ing, Thou art all;

True and faith - ful to the end, Be Thou still my help and guide.
For my guilt Thou didst a - tone, Pur - i - fy me now with - in.
Be my ev - er-pres - ent aid, All - suf - fi - cient grace be - stow.
Keep me in the nar - row way, Lift me when I faint and fall.

CHORUS.

Je - sus all - suf - fi - cient friend, Lead, and com-fort, and de - fend,

All in all I find in thee, Show thy power and grace in me.

No. 46. When My Saviour I Shall See.

Arr. P. B.

P. BILHORN.

1. When my Sav-iour I shall see, In His glo-rious like-ness
2. When I'm whol-ly freed from sin, Spot-less, clean and pure with-
3. When my feet shall press the shore, Trod by an-gel's feet be-
4. Oh, till then be this my care, More His im-age blest to

be, Clad in robes by love sup-plied, Then shall I be sat-is-fied.
in, Meet to stand by Je-sus' side, Then shall I be sat-is-fied.
fore, Near to liv-ing streams that glide, Then shall I be sat-is-fied.
bear; More to con-quer self and pride, So shall I be sat-is-fied.

CHORUS.

Sat-is-fied with love di-vine, Sat-is-fied, since Christ is

mine, Ev-'ry need in Him sup-plied, Then shall I be sat-is-fied.

No. 47.   Seeking the Lost.

W. A. OGDEN.   Luke 15: 6.   W. A. OGDEN.

1. Seek-ing the lost, yes, kind-ly en-treat-ing Wan-der-ers on the mountain a-stray; "Come un-to me," His mes-sage re-peat-ing, Words of the Mas-ter speak-ing to-day.

2. Seek-ing the lost, and point-ing to Je-sus, Souls that are weak, and hearts that are sore; Lead-ing them forth in ways of sal-va-tion, Show-ing the path to life ev-er-more.

3. Thus I would go on mis-sions of mer-cy, Fol-low-ing Christ from day un-to day; Cheer-ing the faint, and rais-ing the fal-len; Point-ing the lost to Je-sus the way.

CHORUS, WITH BASS SOLO.

Go-ing a-far up-on the mountain,
Go-ing a-far............. up-on the moun-tain, Bring-ing the
Bring-ing the wan-d'rer back a-gain, back a-gain.
wan • • d'rer back a-gain.................

By permission.

Seeking the Lost.—Concluded.

In-to the fold of my Re-deem-er,
In - to the fold............ of my Redeem - er,...... Je-sus the

Je - sus, the Lamb for sin - ners slain, for sin - ners slain.
Lamb,.................... for sin - ners slain.................

No. 48. **Cheer Thee.**

" Be not far from me for there is none to help."

Arranged.

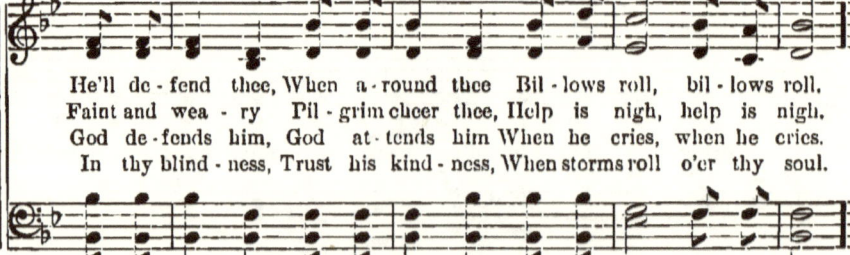

1. God is near thee, There - fore cheer thee, Sad soul, sad soul;
2. Calm thy sad - ness, Look in glad - ness, On high, on high;
3. Mark the sea - bird Wild - ly wheel - ing, Thro' skies, thro' skies;
4. There - fore cheer thee, God is near thee, Sad soul, sad soul;

He'll de - fend thee, When a - round thee Bil - lows roll, bil - lows roll.
Faint and wea - ry Pil - grim cheer thee, Help is nigh, help is nigh.
God de - fends him, God at - tends him When he cries, when he cries.
In thy blind - ness, Trust his kind - ness, When storms roll o'er thy soul.

By permission.

No. 49. What Christ Has Done for Me.

P. B.

P. BILHORN.

1. The Lord has washed a - way my sin,
   The Lord has washed a - way my sin,
2. I'll ne'er for - get the hap - py thought,
   I'll ne'er for - get the hap - py thought,
3. Soon shall I stand be - fore my King,
   Soon shall I stand be - fore my King,
4. Oh, hear the call of Christ the King,
   Oh, hear the call of Christ the King.

For when He knocked I let Him in;
For when He knocked I let Him in;
When first I heard that Christ had bought,
When first I heard that Christ had bought,
His won-drous love and grace to sing,
His won-drous love and grace to sing.
For per - fect peace His word will bring;
For per - fect peace His word will bring;

His pre - cious blood made sin de - part,
His pre - cious blood made sin de - part,
By His own blood my guilt - y soul,
By His own blood my guilt - y soul,
With loved ones who have gone be - fore,
With loved ones who have gone be - fore,
Oh, broth - er, come, He's wait - ing still,
Oh, broth - er, come, He's wait - ing still,

What Christ Has Done for Me—Concluded.

And now He reigns with-in my heart.
And now He reigns with-in my heart.
To cleanse, to save to make me whole.
To cleanse, to save to make me whole.
In heav'n to sing for ev-er-more.
In heav'n to sing for ev-er-more.
Thy heart with joy and peace to fill.
Thy heart with joy and peace to fill.

CHORUS.

Oh, rapturous praise with joy I sing,
rapturous praise, with joy I sing,

For Christ the Lord is now my King,
Christ the Lord, now my King,

I'll en-ter soon the o-pen door,
en-ter soon o-pen door,

rit.

And there I'll sing for ev-er-more.
there I'll sing ev-er-more.

Go, and Sin no more.

Rev. M. Lowrie Hofford.　　　　　　　　　　　Geo. Randall.

mf Marcato.

1. How sweet the gen-tle Sav-ior's voice Up-on the anx-ious ear; Those
2. How sweet the words of heav'n-ly love Like Ser-aph's songs I hear; The
3. "If from the pathway thou should'st stray, I will thy feet re-store; I

REFRAIN. "Thy

words that bid the heart re-joice, And ban-ish ev-ery fear. It
words of melt-ing ten-der-ness, Fall on my list'ning ear. When
came to pit-y not con-demn, Re-pent, and sin no more." Tho'

guilt shall all be washed a-way In my a-ton-ing blood, For

drives the shad-ows from the brow, The bur-den from the heart, To
sor-row fills my soul with gloom, And night o'erspreads the sky, My
weak and sin-ful I may be, And far a-way from God, I'll

"nei-ther do I con-demn thee," Then "Go, and sin no more."

hear Him say, "Come un-to Me, All sin-ful as thou art."
hope, my joy and com-fort spring From wells that nev-er dry.
trust His prom-is-es of grace, And His a-ton-ing blood.

By permission.

Singing of Jesus.

R. M. Offord.   P. Bilhorn.

1. Help me sing my Sav-ior's worth, Help me sing of Je-sus;
2. Sing they may, those sons of light, Round the throne of Je-sus;
3. We can sing the blood He spilt, Pre-cious blood of Je-sus;
4. By His death He set us free, Bless-ed love of Je-sus;

Help me tell His prais-es forth, All who love our Je - sus.
Sing they may, cre - a - tive might, Wondrous might, of Je - sus.
Ran - som from our dread-ful guilt, Praise the blood of Je - sus.
Can our lips now ' si - lent be, Since we've found this Je - sus?

Loud and last - ing be our song, Prais-es to our God be-long;
Sweet - er prais - es we can bring, Rich-er trib-ute to our King,
We can sing the grace that saved, Sing the flood from sin that lav'd,
Oh! re - deem'd ones sing His praise, Sweet est notes of triumph raise,

Round the throne the ser - aph - throng, Sing the praise of Je - sus.
We re - deem - ing love can sing,— Won-drous love of Je - sus.
Sing the love that death hath brav'd,—Migh - ty love of Je - sus.
Bless His name thro' end - less days, Je - sus! Je - sus! Je - sus!

No. 52. In That Land of Bliss.

Miss Julia H. Johnston. P. Bilhorn.

1. In that land of bliss where ho - ly an - gels dwell In the
2. In that sweet new song which saints a - lone can sing, Res - cued
3. Here on earth be - low while wait - ing for that day, Let us
4. Thou art wor - thy, Lord, Thou King of saints be - low, "Just and

pres - ence of the King, We shall gath - er soon, the
ones who once were lost, We shall glad - ly join in
now our lips em - ploy In a song in tune, to
true are all thy ways;" Bring us home at last, life's

CHORUS.

won-drous theme to swell, His re - deem - ing love to sing.
trib - ute to our King, Who re - deemed us at such cost. In that
cheer the up - ward way T'ward the ev - er - last - ing joy.
mys - ter - ies to know, And to Thee shall be the praise.

heav'n - ly land, we shall sing a song, Tell - ing forth His wondrous love;

We shall join the song of the ransom'd throng In the land of bliss a - bove.

No 53. I Could Not Do Without Thee.

Frances R. Havergal.

Sigismund Thalberg, arr.

Andante.

1. I could not do with-out Thee, O Sav-iour of the lost, Whose pre-cious blood re-deemed me At such tre-men-dous cost; Thy right-eous-ness, Thy par-don, Thy pre-cious blood, must be My on-ly hope and com-fort, My glo-ry and my plea,

2. I could not do with-out Thee, I can-not stand a-lone; I have no strength or good-ness, No wis-dom of my own; But Thou, be-lov-ed Sav-iour, Art all in all to me, And weak-ness will be pow-er, If lean-ing hard on Thee.

3. I could not do with-out Thee, For years are fleet-ing fast, And soon in sol-emn si-lence The riv-er must be passed; But Thou wilt nev-er leave me, And, tho' the waves roll high, I know Thou wilt be near me, And whis-per, "It is I."

rit.

No. 54. Manifold Grace.

Mrs. Geo. C. Needham.

P. Bilhorn.

1. As wa - ter cold to faint-ing souls, When fe - ver burns with - in,
2. As wel - come her - alds from a - far, From fields of blood and strife,
3. As joy - ful ti - dings of re - lease, To cap - tives long op - press'd,

The gos - pel like a riv - er rolls, To quench the pow'r of sin.
The gos - pel tells of end - ing war, Of peace, and joy, and life.
The gos - pel makes our bond-age cease, And brings the sin - ner rest.

CHORUS.

O bless - ed news of won - drous pow'r, The mes - sage we re - ceive;

We take free grace this fa - vor'd hour, And on the Lord be - lieve.

Copyright, 1888, by P. Bilhorn.

No. 55. Guide Me, O Thou Great Jehovah!

HARRISON.

1. Guide me, O Thou great Je - hov - ah, Pil-grim thro' this bar - ren land;
2. O - pen now the crys - tal fountain, Whence the heal - ing wa - ters flow;
3. When I tread the verge of Jor - dan, Bid my anx - ious fears sub - side;

I am weak, but Thou art might - y, Hold me with Thy pow'r - ful hand;
Let the fi - er - y, cloud - y pil - lar Lead me all my jour - ney through;
Bear me thro' the swell - ing cur - rent, Land me safe on Ca - naan's side;

Bread of heav - en, Bread of heav - en, Feed me till I want no more.
Strong de - liv - 'rer, Strong de - liv - 'rer, Be Thou still my strength and shield.
Songs of prais - es, Songs of prais - es I will ev - er give to Thee.

Bread of heav - en, Bread of heav - en, Feed me till I want no more.
Strong de - liv - 'rer, Strong de - liv - 'rer, Be Thou still my strength and shield.
Songs of prais - es, Songs of prais - es I will ev - er give to Thee.

By permission.

No. 56. I Love to Sing of Jesus.

" O sing unto the Lord a new song: show forth his salvation from day to day "—Ps. xcvi: 1, 2.

P. B.

1. I love to sing of Je - sus, Who hath redeemed my soul,
2. I love to sing of heav - en, For there my Sav - iour dwells;
3. I love to talk with Je - sus, When bur-dened down with grief;
4. Then, sin - ners, come to Je - sus, Con - fess - ing all your sin:

Whose blood, for me out - pour - ing, Hath cleans'd and made me whole.
And while His grace still keeps me, His bound - less love I'll tell.
I tell Him all my sor - rows, He grants me sweet re - lief.
For now the door is o - pen, He bids you en - ter in.

CHORUS.

Oh, saints, a - rouse and pro - claim it, Come sing this joy - ful strain,

That Je - sus died for sin - ners, And now he lives a - gain.

No. 57. Abiding in Him.

Chas. B. J. Root. Melody by D. C. Wright. Arr.

1. A - bid - ing, oh, so wondrous sweet! I'm rest-ing at the Sav-ior's feet;
2. He speaks, and by his word is given His peace, a rich fore-taste of heav'n!
3. I live; not I; thro' him a - lone By whom the might-y work is done:—
4. Now rest, my heart, the work is done, I'm saved thro' the E - ter - nal son!

I trust in him, I'm sat - is-fied, I'm rest-ing in the Cru - ci - fied!
Not as the world he peace doth give, 'Tis thro' this hope my soul shall live.
Dead to my-self, a - live to him, I count all loss his rest to gain.
Let all my powers my soul em-ploy, To tell the world my peace and joy.

CHORUS.

A - bid - ing, a - bid - ing, Oh! so wondrous sweet!
A - bid-ing in him, I'm rest-ing in him, Oh! so wondrous sweet, wondrous sweet!

I'm rest - ing, rest - ing At the Sav - ior's feet........
I'm rest-ing in him, rest-ing in him, At the Sav - ior's feet, at his feet.

No. 58.

We're on the Way.

Isaiah 35: 8 to 10.

S. M. SAYFORD.

D. B. TOWNER.

1. The promised land! by faith I see, Where God's own glo-ry gilds the day, Where
2. The promised land! where thousands dwell, Who're washed their robes in Je-sus' blood, With
3. The promised land! with gates of pearl, A - jar for all the blood-wash'd throng, A
4. The promised land! with mansions fair, Where Je-sus now pre-pares a place, From
5. The promised land! the Father's house A-waits us on the shining shore, When

we shall dwell with Christ re-deem'd, By His own grace we're on the way.
them we'll wave the branch of palm, When we have cross'd the nar-row flood.
few more march - es—hold on faith! And then we'll sing Re-demption's song.
whence He'll come to take us home, And we shall see Him face to face.
there we'll strike our harps of gold, And praise His name for ev - er - more.

CHORUS.

We're on the way, we're on the way, To glo-ry-land we're on the way; We

fol-low Je-sus day by day, He leads us all a - long the way

No. 59.   Sing Hallelujah to Jesus.

ELIZA M. SHERMAN.   P. BILHORN.

1. Come, sing hal-le-lu-jah to Je-sus, In prais-es so glad and so sweet;
2. Come, sing hal-le-lu-jah to Je-sus, A ran-som He gave for each soul;
3. Come, sing hal-le-lu-jah for-ev-er, The rich-es of Christ's love proclaim

Oh! sing of His grace and His glo-ry, While wor-ship-ing low at His feet.
A fountain He o-pened on Cal-v'ry, Oh! broth-er, come bathe and be whole.
In beau-ty of ho-li-ness wor-ship, Come join in the jub-i-lant strain.

REFRAIN.

Come, sing hal-le-lu-jah for-ev-er, Oh! sing hal-le-lu jah a-gain;

Ho-san-na to God in the high-est, For-ev-er and ev-er, A-men.

No. 60. Is it There? Written There?

"Written in the Lamb's Book of Life."—Rev. 21: 27.

J. E. RANKIN, D. D.   E. S. LORENZ.

1. I do not ask for the pride of earth, For the pride of wealth or the
2. I do not ask for a glo-rious name, That is writ-ten high on the
3. I do not ask that my earth - ly life Should be free from bur - dens and
4. I'd give up all that I hope be - low, All that time can give, or the

pride of birth, Be this, the rath - er, my one great care; In the
scroll of fame, Be this, the rath - er, con-cern of mine, To in-
cares and strife, Nor that its cur - rent have tran - quil flow, If but
world be - stow, If when the Lord in His king - dom come, He will

CHORUS.

Book of Life, that my name is there. In the Book of Life, on those
sure it there, in the book di - vine.
this one thing I may sure - ly know.
know me then and will take me home.

pa - ges fair, Do the an - gels see that my name is there, In the Book of

Life, on those pa - ges fair, Is it there? writ - ten there?
                Is it there? written there?

From "Songs of Grace," by per.

No. 61. Come, Ye Children, March Along.

Miss E. Sherman. P. Bilhorn.

1. Come, ye chil-dren, march a - long, With a stur - dy heart and strong,
2. Are temp-ta-tions in your way? Fight them brave-ly day by day;
3. Are the skies with clouds o'er-cast, Damp and chill - y is the blast?
4. Tho' the hours are dark and sad, Seems there less of good than bad,

With a mer - ry face and song, To the Sav - ior's king - dom.
They will flee from you a - way, At a pray'r to Je - sus.
Oh! the sun - beams will at last, Bright-en all for Je - sus.
Make thy - self and oth - ers glad, With a song of Je - sus.

CHORUS.

Sing-ing, sing-ing on the way, Sing-ing, sing-ing ev-'ry day;

With a mer - ry heart and gay, Sing-ing on the way.

No. 62. Work till the Sun Goes Down.

E. C. A.   (Luke x. 2,)   E. C. Avis

1. Go work in the har-vest of the Lord, And let thy sheaves a-bound,
2. The work is great, the la-borers few, Go spread the news a-round;
3. When souls are dy-ing all a-round, Why sit ye i-dle, dumb?
4. Go work, while the day-light lin-gers, work; Toil on till the crown is won,

Nor stop 'mid the burn-ing heat to rest, But work till the sun goes down.
No lon-ger say there's nought to do, But work till the sun goes down.
Go tell them of a Sav-ior's love, And work till the sun goes down.
And in the vine-yard of the Lord Rest not till the sun goes down.

CHORUS.

Go work, go work, Go work till the sun goes down;
and watch, and pray,

Go forth and work, and watch, and pray, Go work till the sun goes down.

No. 63. What Are You Doing for Jesus?

P. B.

P. BILHORN.

1. Oh, what are you do-ing for Je - sus? He left the bright glories a - bove,
2. Oh, what are you do-ing for Je - sus, Your Sav-ior, Re-deem-er and Friend?
3. Oh, what are you do-ing for Je - sus? All ripen'd the har-vest now stands;
4. Oh, what are you do-ing for Je - sus? While you wait, souls are passing a - way;

And laid down his life as a ran-som, Thy soul to redeem thro' his love.
Are you out in the high-way and hedg-es, Going forth where the Master doth send?
The Lord of the vineyard wants reap-ers, Are you heeding his ur-gent com - mands?
When the Master shall ask for his tal - ents, Oh, brother, what will you then say?

CHORUS.

Oh, what are you do-ing, my broth-er, As the days and the years roll by?

Are you liv-ing for Je-sus who saves you, Are you lay-ing up treasures on high?

No. 64.   Jesus, My All!

Rev. G. D. Watson, D. D.   Wm. J. Kirkpatrick.

1. My heart sings a song From morning till night; A song full of lib-er-ty,
2. My heart hath a rest From sin and from fear; A rest from all doubting, Disap-
3. My heart hath a light In the cloud-i-est day; A light which illumines Each
4. My heart hath a Friend, All compassion and love, Whose speech falls as soft As the

Love, and of light: A song of the Ca-naan-land, Hap-py and bright, And
point-ment and care: A rest like the sky, Bend-ing calm o'er the year,—And
mo-ment my way: A light which will not let The lit-tle one stray,—And
star-light a-bove: A friend that a-bid-eth, And will not re-move,—And

REFRAIN.

all of my *song* is Je-sus.   Je-sus, Je-sus, All of my song is Je-sus:
all of my *rest* is Je-sus.   Je-sus, Je-sus, All of my rest is Je-sus:
all of my *light* is Je-sus.   Je-sus, Je-sus, All of my light is Je-sus:
that dearest *friend* is Je-sus.   Je-sus, Je-sus, That dearest friend is Je-sus:

From morn-ing till night I sing with de-light,— Je-sus, my pre-cious Je-sus!

From "Songs of Joy and Gladness," by per.

No. 65. Shall I Meet my Sainted Mother?

The writer of these words in childhood promised his dying mother that he would meet her in heaven. Forgetful of his promise, he on reaching manhood became an infidel. The stirring words of Evangelist "Schiverea" brought to mind the long forgotten teaching of that Christian mother, and casting aside his infidelity he accepted Christ as his Savior.

GEORGE THOMPSON.   P. BILHORN.

1. Shall I meet my saint-ed moth-er, In her home be-yond the skies?
2. When the bells of heav-en ring-ing, Wake the an-gel's song a-gain,
3. All the years of sin and sor-row, That I've suf-fer'd since she died,

Will I see the love-light beam-ing, From her ten-der lov-ing eyes?
For the wan-der-er re-turn-ing From the paths of sin and pain,
Will be van-ish'd on that mor-row, When I stand by moth-er's side,

Will she know me when I meet her, For I'm changed so sad-ly now?
Will my moth-er there be wait-ing, Wait-ing with her look so mild?
Stand with her be-fore the Sav-ior, There a-mong the blood-wash'd throng,

Will she see her fair-haired dar-ling In this old and wrin-kled brow?
Will she press me to her bo-som, As she did when but a child?
Join-ing in the heav'n-ly rapt-ure Of the glad re-demp-tion song

No. 66. Trust Jesus Over All.

P. H. ROBLIN.   P. BILHORN.

1. O trust the Sav-ior, let come what may, Trust in his word so true;
2. When sore-ly tempt-ed in sin to stray, Look up to Christ a-lone;
3. When tears of sor-row be-gin to fall, And sad-ness fills the soul;

His gra-cious promise your heart shall stay, His strength shall bear you through.
He keeps his chil-dren up-on the way, As they keep near the throne.
O then re-mem-ber, he knows it all, On Him thy bur-den roll.

CHORUS.

O trust Him then through life and death, Thro' tri-als great and small; (and small;)

Let come what may, till lat-est breath, Trust Je-sus o-ver all.

No. 67. The Child of a King!

"Heirs of the kingdom."—James 2: 5.

HATTIE E. BUELL.

JOHN B. SUMNER, arr.

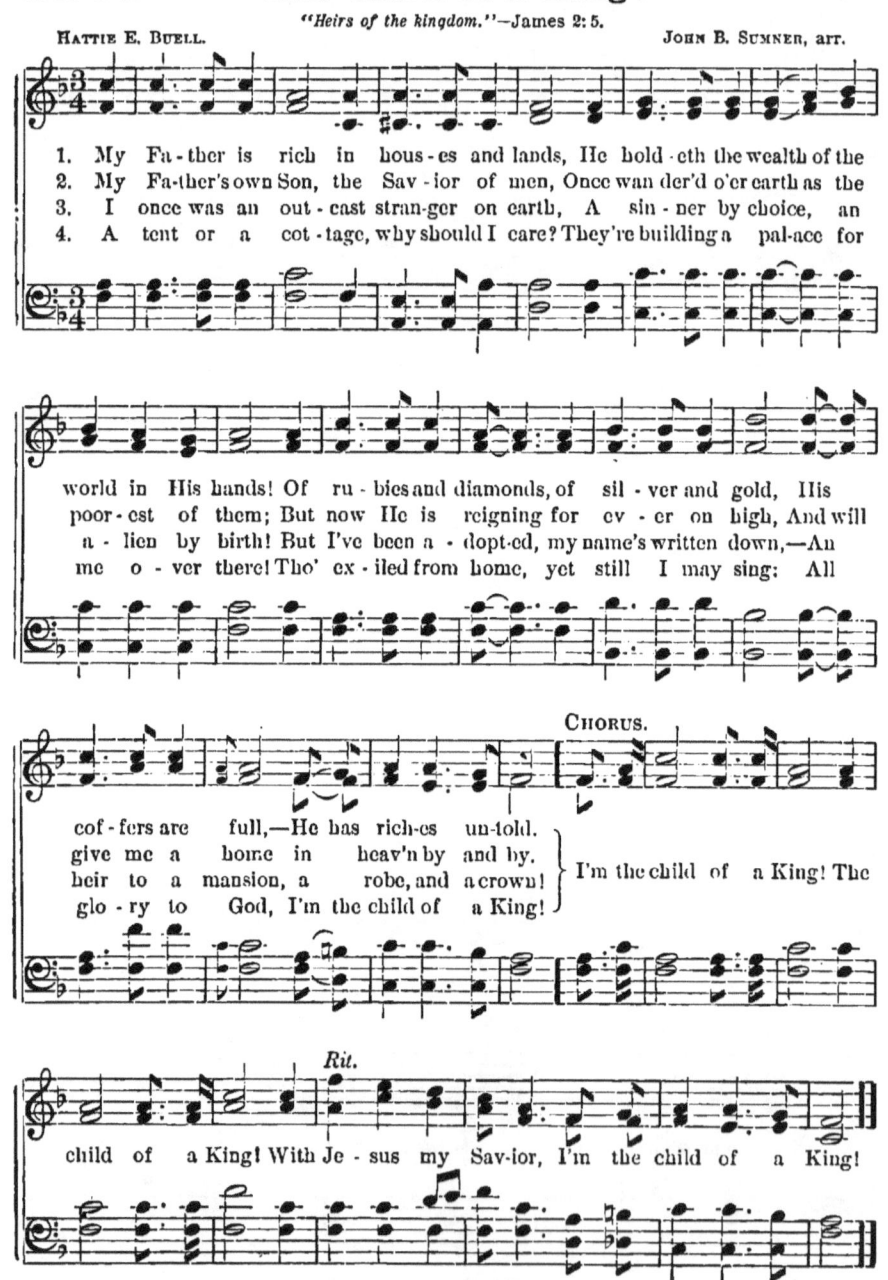

1. My Fa-ther is rich in hous-es and lands, He hold-eth the wealth of the
2. My Fa-ther's own Son, the Sav-ior of men, Once wan-der'd o'er earth as the
3. I once was an out-cast stran-ger on earth, A sin-ner by choice, an
4. A tent or a cot-tage, why should I care? They're building a pal-ace for

world in His hands! Of ru-bies and diamonds, of sil-ver and gold, His
poor-est of them; But now He is reigning for ev-er on high, And will
a-lien by birth! But I've been a-dopt-ed, my name's written down,—An
me o-ver there! Tho' ex-iled from home, yet still I may sing: All

cof-fers are full,—He has rich-es un-told.
give me a home in heav'n by and by.
heir to a mansion, a robe, and a crown!
glo-ry to God, I'm the child of a King!

CHORUS.

I'm the child of a King! The
child of a King! With Je-sus my Sav-ior, I'm the child of a King!

Rit.

Permission by John B. Sumner.

No. 68. A Story Sweet and True.

E. W. OAKES. P. BILHORN.

1. We'll sing the won-drous sto-ry, 'Tis ev-er sweet and true;
2. The cru-el world, they took Him, With thorns they crowned His head;
3. His friends whom He loved dear-ly, And whom He died to save,
4. My Lord now reigns in glo-ry He's com-ing soon for me;

Of Je-sus' love so pre-cious, Now free-ly of-fered you;
And then to Calvary's mount-ain The pre-cious Lamb was led;
They begged His pre-cious bod-y, And laid it in the grave;
And then with all the ran-somed, His glo-rious face I'll see;

He left the joys of heav-en, His Fa-ther's home on high,
The nails of shame were driv-en, The blood flow'd from His side;
But God, His Fa-ther, raised him, Tri-umph-ant, from the dead;
And shout, be-hold the bride-groom, Put on your gar-ments fair,

For lost and ru-in'd sin-ners, To suf-fer and to die.
He cried, O God, for-give them, And bowed his head and died.
Oh! glo-ry hal-le-lu-jah, Now death is cap-tive led.
And go ye out to meet Him, With rapt-ure in the air.

Copyright, 1886, by P. BILHORN.

No. 69. Behold Me Standing at the Door!

E. J. CROSBY.   MRS. J. F. KNAPP.

With feeling. (May be sung as a Solo.)

1. Be - hold Me standing at the door, And hear Me pleading ev - er - more,
2. I bore the cru - el thorns for thee, I wait - ed long and pa - tient - ly:
3. I would not plead with thee in vain; Re - mem - ber all My grief and pain;
4. I bring thee joy from heaven above, I bring thee pardon, peace, and love:

With gen - tle voice: oh, heart of sin, May I come in? may I come in?
Say, wea - ry heart, oppressed with sin, May I come in? may I come in?
I died to ran - som thee from sin; May I come in? may I come in?
Say, wea - ry heart, oppressed with sin, May I come in? may I come in?

REFRAIN.

Be - hold Me standing at the door, And hear Me pleading ev - er - more: Say,

wea - ry heart, oppressed with sin, May I come in? May I come in?

By permission.

No. 70. God's Wonderful Love.

P. B. JOHN iii. 16. P. BILHORN.

1. Hast thou heard of God, who in wondrous love, Gave his on - ly Son to die;
2. It was love that gave, it was love that came, When the Lord ap-pear'd to men;
3. I was won to Christ by this wondrous love, Oh, the love of God to me;
4. By the love that sought, by the love that bought, By the grace God sends so free;

Died that we might live, yes, for - ev - er-more, In a home pre-par'd on high.
On the cru - el cross Je - sus died in love, There to save us from our sin.
For it filled my soul, and it made me whole, It has cleans'd and made me free.
All who Christ re - ceive, and on him be-lieve, They shall live e - ter - nal - ly.

CHORUS.

It was won-der-ful love, Oh, such wonderful love, God's love in Christ made nigh;

It was won-der-ful love, Oh, yes, matchless love, That brought Christ here to die.

No. 71. O Prodigal, Don't Stay Away.

"I will arise and go to my Father."—Luke 15: 18.

J. E. RANKIN, D. D.   J. W. BISCHOFF.

1. O prod-i-gal, don't stay a-way! The Fa-ther is wait-ing to day; There's
2. O prod-i-gal brother, come home! Why longer in wretchedness roam? You're
3. O prod-i-gal, what will you do? Love's ta-ble is wait-ing for you; For-
4. O prod-i-gal broth-er, a-rise! For par-don, look up to the skies; No

room and to spare, There is rai-ment to wear, O prod-i-gal, don't stay a-way.
lone-ly and lost, You are driv-en and toss'd, O prod-i-gal broth-er, come home.
giveness so sweet, Sure, your coming will greet, O prod-i-gal, what will you do?
long-er then stray From thy Fa-ther a-way, O prod-i-gal broth-er, a-rise.

CHORUS.

Will you come?.......... Will you come?.......... Will you
Will you come?   Will you come?

come, come home to - day?   There is wel-come for you, There's a
                    Will you come?

kiss, kind and true, Then, O prod-i-gal, don't stay a-way.

From "Gospel Bells," by per.

No. 72. Come Unto Me Saith Jesus.

Miss Julia H. Johnston.

P. Bilhorn.

1. "Come un-to me," saith the cru-ci-fied One, My blood I shed, My life I give." Hark! He is ris-en from death and the grave, "Come un-to me and live."
2. All who are sad and for-sak-en, give heed, The sick the poor, the lost and blind, Com-fort and par-don and heal-ing you need, Oh! come and you shall find.
3. All who are walk-ing in sun-shine to-day, The glad and free, un-touched by care, Je-sus is call-ing to come while you may, His great-er joy to share.
4. Je-sus, Re-deem-er, we come un-to Thee, We hear Thy voice, Thy lov-ing voice, Keep and de-fend us and teach us Thy way, And make us to re-joice.

Chorus.

"Come un-to me, oh come un-to me, 'Tis life ev-er-last-ing I give,"...... Then I give. come, wea-ry one, while yet he calls, For-ev-er with Him to live.

No. 73. The Lily of the Valley.

English Melody.

1. I have found a friend in Je-sus, He's ev-'ry-thing to me, He's the
2. He all my griefs has ta-ken, and all my sor-rows borne; In temp-
3. He will nev-er, nev-er leave me, nor yet for-sake me here, While I

fair-est of ten thou-sand to my soul; The Lil-y of the Val-ley, in
ta-tion He's my strong and might-y tow'r; I have all for Him for-sa-ken, and
live by faith and do His bless-ed will; A wall of fire a-bout me, I've

D. S. *Lil-y of the Val-ley, the*

FINE.

Him a-lone I see All I need to cleanse and make me ful-ly whole.
all my i-dols torn From my heart, and now He keeps me by His power
nothing now to fear, With His man-na He my hun-gry soul shall fill.

bright and Morn-ing Star, He's the fair-est of ten thou-sand to my soul.

In sor-row He's my com-fort, in troub-le He's my stay,
Tho' all the world for-sake me, and Sa-tan tempts me sore,
Then sweep-ing up to glo-ry, to see His bless-ed face,

D.S.

He tells me ev-'ry care on Him to roll. He's the
Thro' Je-sus I shall safe-ly reach the goal. (Hallelujah!) He's the
Where riv-ers of de-light shall ev-er roll. He's the

No. 74. Behold Him hanging.

E. C. A.

E. C. Avis.

1. On the cross the Saviour hang-ing, Bled and died for you and me;
2. O, the blood stain'd cross of Je - sus, How it fills my soul with peace,
3. 'Tis in - deed a truth most precious, That for sin - ners Je - sus died,

Wondrous love! Oh! who can know it, Boundless, price-less, full and free.
As I there be - hold him dy - ing, Bring-ing nought but my - re lease.
And we have a full re - mis - sion Through a Sav - iour cru - ci - fied.

Chorus.

On the cross,............ be-hold him hang - ing,

On the cross, be-hold him hang-ing, On the cross, be-hold him hanging,

On the blood . . . stain'd cross for me;..............

On the cross, the blood stain'd cross, On the cross, the blood-stain'd cross.

Je - sus died.............. to bring sal - va - tion,

Je - sus died to bring sal - va - tion, Je - sus died to bring sal - va - tion,

Behold Him hanging. Concluded.

Je - sus died for you and me.

Je - sus died, Je - sus died for you and me.

No. 75. Revive Us Again.

Dr. W. P. MACKAY.

English Melody.

1. We praise Thee, O God! for the Son of Thy love, For
2. We praise Thee, O God! for Thy Spir - it of light, Who has
3. All glo - ry and praise to the Lamb that was slain, Who has

CHORUS.

Je - sus who died, and is now gone a - bove. Hal - le - lu - ja!
shown us our Sav - ior, and scat - tered our night. Hal - le - lu - ja!
borne all our sins, and has cleansed ev - 'ry stain. Hal - le - lu - ja!

Thine the glo - ry, Hal - le - lu - jah! A - men. Re - vive us a - gain.

4. All glory and praise to the God of all grace,
   Who has bought us, and sought us, and guided our ways.

5. Revive us again; fill each heart with Thy love;
   May each soul be rekindled with fire from above.

No. 76. Jesus, My Savior.

"Wash me thoroughly from mine iniquity, and cleanse me from my sin."—Ps. li. 2.

G. A. WILSON.   P. BILHORN.

1. Je-sus, my Sav-ior, to Thee I come, Tho' wretched, vile, thou dost not shun;
2. Je-sus, my Sav-ior, to Thee I pray, Wash all my sins and guilt a-way;
3. Je-sus, Thy word I do be-lieve, And all Thy prom-is-es re-ceive;
4. Je-sus, my all, I now re-sign, Since par-don thro' thy grace is mine;

For who so com-eth thou hast taught, Thou wilt in no wise cast him out.
Lord, cleanse me now from ev-'ry stain, For there is pow-er in thy name.
Lord, now my-self to Thee I give, And in Thee ev-er-more shall live.
Thy name I'll ev-er-more re-peat Be-fore my Fa-ther's mer-cy-seat.

CHORUS.

Him that com-eth, Him that com-eth, Him that com-eth to
me, (to me,) I will in no wise, I will in
no wise, I will in no wise, in no wise cast him out.

No. 77. Let the Savior In.

" If any man hear my voice, and open the door, I will come in to him."—Rev. 3: 20.

Rev. J. B. ATCHINSON.　　　　　　　　　　　　　　　　E. O. EXCELL.

1. There's a Stran-ger at the door: Let　Him in!
2. O - pen now to Him your heart: Let　Him in!
3. Hear you now His lov - ing voice? Let　Him in!
4. Now ad - mit the heav'nly Guest: Let　Him in!

Let the Savior in! Let the Savior in!

He has been there oft be - fore: Let　Him in!
If you wait He will de - part: Let　Him in!
Now, oh, now make Him your choice: Let　Him in!
He will make for you a feast: Let　Him in!

Let the Savior in! Let the Savior in!

Let Him in, ere He is gone; Let Him in, the Ho - ly One,
Let Him in; He is your Friend; He your soul will sure de - fend;
He is stand-ing at the door; Joy to you He will re - store,
He will speak your sins for - giv'n, And when earth - ties all are riv'n,

Je-sus Christ, the Fa-ther's Son: Let　Him in!
He will keep you to the end: Let　Him in!
And His name you will a - dore: Let　Him in!
He will take you home to heav'n: Let　Him in!

Let the Savior in! Let the Savior in!

No. 78.

I Do Believe.

" Without shedding of blood is no remission." — Heb. ix: 22.

P. B.

P. BILHORN.

1. I do believe with all my soul That Je-sus' blood now makes me whole!
2. I do believe with all my heart That Je-sus doth new life impart!
3. I do believe that Christ my King Will come a-gain me home to bring!
4. I do believe in heav'n a-bove There will be naught but pur-est love;

I plunge be-neath the crim-son tide, Which flow'd from out His wounded side!
For now I live as ne'er be-fore, In Christ who liv-eth ev-er-more
To dwell in man-sions bright and fair, And with Him in His glo-ry share.
And there my ran-som'd soul shall sing, Ho-san-na to my God and King!

CHORUS.

I do be-lieve! I do be-lieve! The cleans-ing blood I now re-ceive;

With joy my ransom'd soul doth sing Ho-san-nas to my God and King.

Yield not to Temptation.

Words and music by H. R. PALMER.

1. Yield not to temp-ta-tion, For yield-ing is sin, Each vic-t'ry will
2. Shun e - vil com-pan-ions, Bad lan-guage dis - dain, God's name hold in
3. To him that o'er-com-eth, God giv - eth a crown, Thro' faith we shall

help you Some oth - er to win; Fight man-ful - ly on - ward,
rev-'rence, Nor take it in vain; Be thought-ful and earn - est,
con - quer, Tho' of - ten cast down; He who is our Sav - ior,

Dark pas - sions sub - due, Look ev - er to Je - sus, He'll car - ry you through.
Kind-heart-ed and true, Look ev - er to Je - sus, He'll car - ry you through.
Our strength will re - new, Look ev - er to Je - sus, He'll car - ry you through.

CHORUS.

Ask the Sav - ior to help you, Com - fort, strengthen and keep you;

He is will - ing to aid you, He will car - ry you through.

No. 80. Rouse, Ye Saints.

C. H. YATMAN. P. BILHORN.

1. Rouse, ye saints, the world is dy-ing, We must work while it is day;
2. Wake, ye men, let us be do-ing, While the sun is in the sky;
3. Je-sus, Sav-ior, help our spir-its, That we nev-er wea-ry be

Sin-ners lost to us are cry-ing For the strait and nar-row way.
Let us seek the weak and er-ring, Pre-cious souls that soon may die.
Lead-ing sin-ners to the Fount-ain Ev-er flow-ing, full and free.

CHORUS.

We will work from morn till night, By the Spir-it's pow'r and might,

Lead-ing men un-to the Light, Bless-ed Light of Day!

No. 81. The Cleansing Wave.

"And washed us from our sins in his own blood."—Rev. 13 : 5.

MRS. PHŒBE PALMER.

MRS. JOS. F. KNAPP.

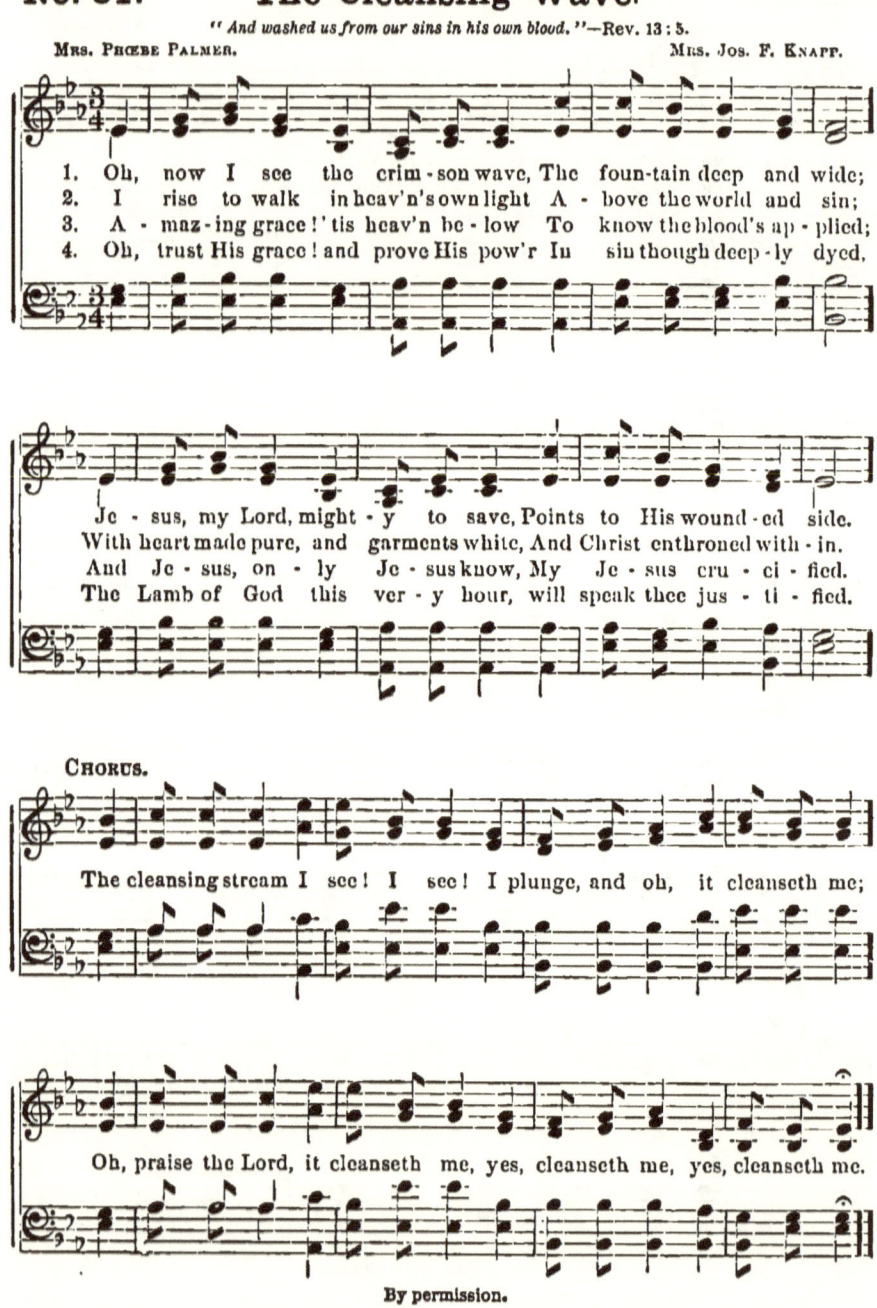

1. Oh, now I see the crim-son wave, The foun-tain deep and wide;
2. I rise to walk in heav'n's own light A - bove the world and sin;
3. A - maz-ing grace! 'tis heav'n be - low To know the blood's ap - plied;
4. Oh, trust His grace! and prove His pow'r In sin though deep - ly dyed,

Je - sus, my Lord, might - y to save, Points to His wound - ed side.
With heart made pure, and garments white, And Christ enthroned with - in.
And Je - sus, on - ly Je - sus know, My Je - sus cru - ci - fied.
The Lamb of God this ver - y hour, will speak thee jus - ti - fied.

CHORUS.

The cleansing stream I see! I see! I plunge, and oh, it cleanseth me;

Oh, praise the Lord, it cleanseth me, yes, cleanseth me, yes, cleanseth me.

By permission.

No. 82. While the Years are Rolling by.

P. B.
P. BILHORN.

1. There is work that we can do, While the years roll by; For the
2. Lis-ten to the Mas-ter's call, While the years roll by; Ho! ye
3. It may be your joy to win, While the years roll by; Some-one

la-b'rers are but few, While the years roll by; Let us
reap-ers, one and all, While the years roll by; Do not
from the path of sin, While the years roll by; To your

work and watch and pray, Till the crown-ing day, While the years are
i - dly wait-ing stand, Heed the Lord's command, While the years are
trust be firm and true, God de-pends on you, While the years are

CHORUS.

roll - ing by. While the years (while the years) are roll - ing

by, (roll - ing by) While the years, (while the years) are roll - ing

While the Years are Rolling by.—Concluded.

by   (roll - ing   by)   There   is   work   that   we   can

do,   While   the   years   are   roll - ing   by.   (roll - ing by.)

No. 83.   The Lord's my Shepherd.

"Rous' Version," 1649.   MOZART.

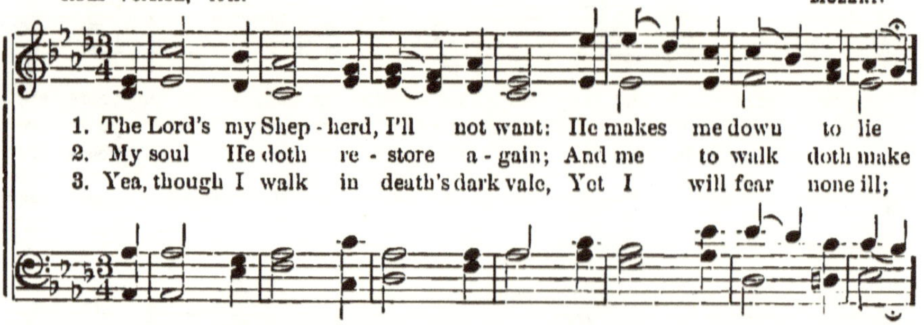

1. The Lord's my Shep - herd, I'll   not want: He makes   me down   to lie
2. My soul He doth   re - store a - gain; And me   to walk   doth make
3. Yea, though I walk   in death's dark vale, Yet I   will fear   none ill;

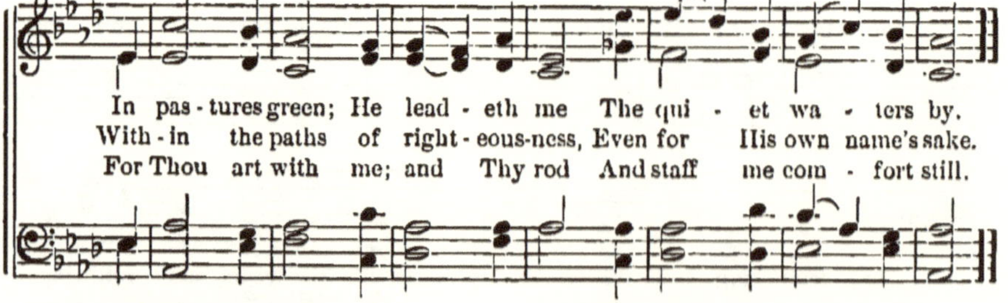

In pas - tures green; He lead - eth me   The qui - et wa - ters by.
With - in   the paths   of right - eous-ness, Even for   His own name's sake.
For Thou   art with   me; and   Thy rod   And staff   me com - fort still.

4 My table Thou hast furnishéd
In presence of my foes;
My head Thou dost with oil annoint,
And my cup overflows.

5 Goodness and mercy all my life
Shall surely follow me;
And in God's house for evermore
My dwelling-place shall be,

No. 84. Memories of Galilee.

"Jesus walked in Galilee."—John 7: 1.

Robert Morris, LL. D.　　　　　　　　　　　　　　　　H. R. Palmer.

1. Each coo-ing dove　and sigh-ing bough,　That makes the eve so blest to me, Has something far di-vin-er now, It bears me back to Gal-i-lee.

2. Each flowery glen　and moss-y dell,　Where hap-py birds in song a-gree, Thro' sun-ny morn the prais-es tell, Of sights and sounds in Gal-i-lee.

3. And when I read　the thrilling lore　Of him who walked up-on the sea, I long, oh, how I long once more, To fol-low him in Gal-i-lee.

Chorus.

O Gal-i-lee! sweet Gal-i-lee! Where Je-sus loved so much to be; O Gal-i-lee! blue Gal-i-lee! Come, sing thy song a-gain to me!

No. 85.   Christ is Born.

ELIZA M. SHERMAN.

P. BILHORN.

1. List to the music over the earth, Loud the merry joy-bells
2. Peace he is bring-ing, good-will to men, Gifts of grace and glo-ry,
3. Soon will the day-star shin-ing so bright, Turn the gloom to glo-ry,—
4. Oh! star of beau-ty' light up the way, Where thy glo-ry shin-eth

tell of Je-sus' birth; Join in the mu-sic, for on this morn,
tell it once a-gain; O may our hearts for love, Lord, of thee,
dark-ness in-to light; Glad hal-le-lu-jah sing on this morn,
from the gates of day: And in our hearts this bright Christ-mas morn,

CHORUS.

Christ, our Lord and King is born.
One e-ter-nal Christ-mas be.
For our Sav-ior, King is born.
May our Lord and King be born.

Glo-ry in the high-est,

glo-ry give to-day, Tell the bless-ed sto-ry, sound a-loud the lay;

Ring out the tid-ings for on this morn, Christ, our Lord and King is born.

No. 86. In Sight of the Crystal Sea.

Rev. J. E. Rankin, D. D.   *"Son, Remember."*—Luke 16: 25.   J. W. Bischoff, by Per.

1. I sat a - lone with life's mem - o - ries In sight of the crys - tal
2. I thought me then of my childhood days, The prayer at my moth - er's
3. I thought, I thought of the days of God I'd wast - ed in fol - ly and
4. I heard a voice, like the voice of God: "Re - mem - ber, re - mem - ber, my

sea, And I saw the throne of the star - crown'd ones, With
knee; Of the coun - sels grave that my fa - ther gave—The
sin— Of the times I'd mock'd when the Sav - ior knock'd, And
son! Re - mem - ber thy ways in the form - er days, The

nev - er a crown for me; And then the voice of the
wrath I was warn'd to flee; I said "Is it then, too
I would not let Him in; I thought, I thought of the
crown that thou mightst have won!" I thought, I thought, and my

Judge said, Come, Of the Judge on the great white throne; And I
late, too late? Shut with - out must I stand for aye?" And the
vows I made, When I lay at death's dark door— Would He
thoughts ran on, Like the tide of a sun - less sea— "Am I

saw the star-crown'd take their seats, But none could I call my own.
Judge, will He say, "I know you not," Howe'er I may knock and pray?
spare my life, I'd give up the strife, And serve Him for - ev - er - more."
liv - ing or dead?" to my - self I said, "An end is there ne'er to be?"

In Sight of the Crystal Sea.—Concluded.

5 It seemed as tho' I woke from a dream,
　How sweet was the light of day!
Melodious sounded the Sabbath bells
　From towers that were far away;
I then became as a little child,
　And I wept and wept afresh;
For the Lord had taken my heart of stone,
　And given a heart of flesh.

6 Still oft I sit with life's memories,
　And I think of the crystal sea;　[ones,
And I see the thrones of the star-crown'd
　I know there's a crown for me; ["Come,"
And when the voice of the Judge says,
　Of the Judge on the great white throne,
I know 'mid the thrones of the star-crown'd
　There's one I shall call my own.　[ones,

No. 87.　　　Closer, Lord, to Thee.

"It is good for me to draw near to God."—Ps. 73: 28.

E. G. Taylor, D. D.　Alt.　　　　　　　　　　　Geo. C. Stebbins.

1. Clos - er, Lord, to Thee I cling, Clos - er still to Thee;
2. Clos - er yet, O Lord, my Rock, Ref - uge of my soul;
3. Clos - er still, my Help, my Stay, Clos - er, clos - er still;
4. Clos - er, Lord, to Thee I come, Light of life di - vine;

Safe be - neath Thy shelter-ing wing I would ev - er be;
Dread I not the tem - pest-shock, Tho' the bil - lows roll.
Meek - ly there I learn to say, "Fa - ther, not my will;"
Thro' the ev - er bless - ed Son, Joy and peace are mine;

Rude the blast of doubt and sin, Fierce as - saults with-out, with - in,
Wild - est storm can - not a - larm, For to me can come no harm,
Learn that in af - flic - tion's hour, When the clouds of sor - row lower,
Let me in Thy love a - bide, Keep me ev - er by Thy side,

Help me, Lord, the bat - tle win;—Clos - er, Lord, to Thee.
Lean - ing on Thy lov - ing arm;—Clos - er, Lord, to Thee.
Love di - rects Thy hand of power;—Clos - er, Lord, to Thee.
In the "Rock of A - ges" hide,—Clos - er, Lord, to Thee.

No. 88. On the Cross.

Words for chorus arr: P. BILHORN;

1. A - las! and did my Sav - ior bleed? and did my Sov - 'reign die?
2. Was it for crimes that I had done, He groan'd up - on the tree?
3. But drops of grief can ne'er re - pay the debt of love I owe;

Would He de - vote that sa - cred head, For such a worm as I?
A - maz - ing pi - ty! grace un-known! And love be - yond de - gree!
Here, Lord! I give my - self to thee, 'Tis all that I can do.

CHORUS. *Faster.*

On the cross, on the cross where I first saw my Lord, And the

bur - den of my heart roll'd a - way (roll'd a - way.) It was

there by faith I received His word and now I am happy all the day,

No. 89.   Spurn Me Not.

REV. J. H. MARTIN.   D. E. DORTCH.

1. Spurn me not, O lov-ing Sav-ior, Cast me not a-way?
2. I am sin-ful, vile, un-worth-y, All un-clean I am;
3. Thou hast died for me a ran-som, Shed thy pre-cious blood;
4. To thy cross my soul is cling-ing, There my faith is stay'd;

Grant me par-don, life and fa-vor, For thy grace I pray.
Thou art righteous, pure and ho-ly, Spot-less, per-fect Lamb.
Thou hast pur-chas'd full re-demp-tion, Bought my peace with God.
Make me joy-ful, ev-er sing-ing, "Thou my debt hast paid."

CHORUS.

Je-sus, Sav-ior, Cast me not a-way,
Bless-ed Je-sus, lov-ing Sav-ior,

For I seek thy smile and fa-vor; Hear me while I pray,

By permission.

No. 90. Be Strong in Jehovah.

Arr from G. & T.   P. BILHORN.

1. Be strong in Je - ho - vah, though hard be the fight, We'll
2. We'll sing while we march through the midst of our foes, Who
3. Thus armed we shall stand and shall meet Sa - tan's wiles; We
4. The trum - pet is sound - ing, the trum - pet of war, Not

con - quer, we know, in the power of His might; Put
stand all de - ter - mined our way to op - pose; We'll
know his de - vi - ces, the world he be - guiles, 'Tis
peace while we wait for our bright morn - ing star; We

on the whole ar - mour of God, ev - 'ry one, Let
con - quer their le - gion, our bat - tle song raise; The
not a - gainst flesh and the blood that we fight, But
watch where the foe would a - larm or sur - prise; The

Repeat pp.

Christ be your cap - tain till vic - t'ry is won.
Lord is our cap - tain; His name ev - er praise.
powers that would force us from heav - en - ly light.
trum - pet is sound - ing; a - rise, then a - rise.

No. 91.   Rise, and let me in.

" Behold, I stand at the door and knock."—Rev. iii : 20.

W. A. O.

N. E. TOWNSEND.

Andante.

1. Lo! a stran-ger stand - ing there, Knocking, knock-ing at the door,
2. 'Tis thy Sav-iour wait - ing there, Knocking, knock-ing at the door,
3. Hear the Sav-iour call to - day Knocking, knock-ing at the door;
4. Shall thy Sav-iour plead in vain, Knocking, knock-ing at the door?

Love - ly stran-ger, won-d'rous fair, Knock-ing, knocking at the door;
Call - ing thee, oh wan - der - er, Knock ing, knocking at the door;
Do not grieve thy Lord a - way, Knock-ing, knocking at the door.
Will you slight His call a - gain, Knock-ing, knocking at the door?

Wait - ing, oh! so pa - tient-ly, Call - ing oh! so ten - der-ly,
Plead - ing, oh! so ear - nest - ly, Striv - ing oh! so faith - ful - ly,
Wea - ry, worn, and troub - led breast, Tempt - ed one, with care op - prest,
Will you heed His ear - nest plea? "Hea - vy la - den, come to me."

O - pen now thy heart to me; Oh, rise, and let me in.
Tis thy Sav - iour calls to thee; Oh, rise, and let me in.
I will give thy spir - it rest; Oh, rise, and let me in.
Rest and peace I give to thee; Oh, rise, and let me in.

By permission.

No. 92. My Jesus, I love Thee.

" Mine are thine and thine are mine."—John 17 : 10.

London Hymn Book, 1864.   A. J. GORDON. By per.

1. My Jesus, I love Thee, I know Thou art mine,
2. I love Thee, be-cause Thou hast first lov-éd me,
3. I will love Thee in life, I will love Thee in death
4. In man-sions of glo - ry and end - less de-light,

For Thee all the fol - lies of sin I re - sign;
And pur - chased my par - don on Cal - va - ry's tree;
And praise Thee as long as Thou lend - est me breath;
I'll ev - er a - dore Thee in heav - en so bright;

My gra - cious Re - deem - er, my Sav - iour art Thou,
I love Thee for wear - ing the thorns on Thy brow;
And say when the death - dew lies cold on my brow,
I'll sing with the glit - ter - ing crown on my brow,

If ev - er I loved Thee, my Je - sus, 'tis now.

What Time I am Afraid.

What time I am afraid, I will trust in Thee. Ps. 56 : 3.

Miss J. H. Johnston.   "Scotch." Arr. by P. Bilhorn.

1. Some times the sky is o-ver-cast, I fear to lose my way;
2. Ac-cu-sing Conscience, like a flame, With-in my spir-it burns,
3. From all the un-known fut-ure days, My tim-id heart re-coils,
4. When twi-light shad-ows soft-ly fall, And night comes on a-pace,

Un-til the storm be o-ver-past, O keep me safe I pray.
The tempt-er speaks of wrath and shame, My soul in an-guish turns.
But known to God are all my ways, And all my cares and toils.
In life and death, O Lord of all, I would be-hold Thy face.

In dark-ness, dan-ger, and in doubt, My heart is sore dis-mayed,
To Him whose blood a-tones for me, On whom my heart is stayed,
The wis-dom, pow'r, and might are Thine, But mine the prom-ised aid,
The fi-nal hour, Oh! let me meet In peace, and un-dis-mayed,

But "I will trust in Thee O Lord, What time I am a-fraid."
For "I will trust in Thee O Lord, What time I am a-fraid."
And "I will trust in Thee O Lord, What time I am a-fraid."
For "I will trust in Thee O Lord, What time I am a-fraid."

Take the Step.

Mary More.   J. H. Burke,

1. Broth-er, at the threshold stand ing, See you not the o-pen door,
2. See the ban-quet hall of mer-cy, See thy seat that va-cant stands,
3. Keep thy Lord no long-er wait-ing, He hath died, thy soul to win,
4. Just a step, will you not take it, While in pray'r to God we bow,

See you not the hand ex-tend-ed, Reach-ing out to help you o'er?
Think of loved ones wait ing for thee, See them now with beckoning hands.
Let His love, thy heart constraining, Lead thee now to en-ter in.
Will you not your sins for-sak-ing, Trust in Christ, and trust him now?

Chorus.

Take the step,............ my broth-er, take it,
Oh, take the step, my broth-er, take it,

Take the step............... and yield to God;...............
Oh, take the step, and yield to God,

Rise and Christ........... con-fess as Sav-ior,
A-rise, and Christ con-fess as Sav-ior,

Take The step. Concluded

Take the step......... .... and trust his word, and trust his word.

Oh, take the step,

No. 95. As I am, O Jesus, Take me.

MARY MORE.   J. H. BURKE.

1. As I am, O Je-sus, take me, I no long-er will re-bel;
2. Take me, Lord, as Thou hast found me, Guilt-y, vile and far from Thee,
3. Break me, Lord, from love of sin - ing, Break, O break my stub-born will,
4. Make me, Lord, what thou would'st have me, Make me like Thy-self to be,

Let thy ho - ly Spir - it break me, And with - in me ev - er dwell.
Sa-tan's fet - ters fast-ened round me, Take me, Lord, and make me free.
Now the work of grace be-gin-ning, Let Thy love my spi - it fill.
Make me pure and make me ho - ly, Con - se - cra - ted un - to Thee.

CHORUS.

As I am, O Je-sus, take me, Here I give my-self to Thee;

Sav-ior, take me, break, and make me, All that Thou would'st have me be

No. 96. What will you now Do with Jesus.

Matthew 27:22.

P. B.

P. BILHORN.

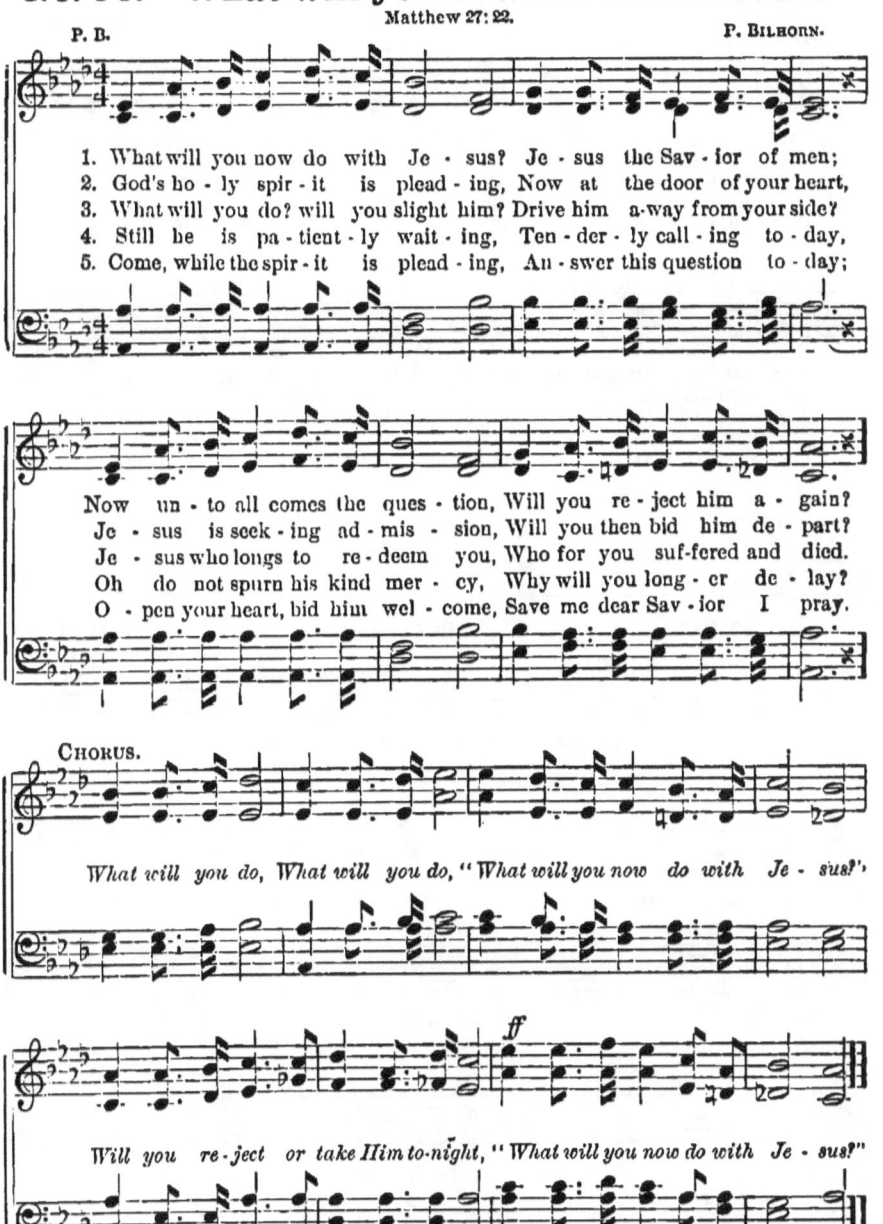

1. What will you now do with Je - sus? Je - sus the Sav - ior of men;
2. God's ho - ly spir - it is plead - ing, Now at the door of your heart,
3. What will you do? will you slight him? Drive him a-way from your side?
4. Still he is pa - tient-ly wait - ing, Ten - der-ly call - ing to - day,
5. Come, while the spir - it is plead - ing, An - swer this question to - day;

Now un - to all comes the ques - tion, Will you re - ject him a - gain?
Je - sus is seek-ing ad - mis - sion, Will you then bid him de - part?
Je - sus who longs to re - deem you, Who for you suf-fered and died.
Oh do not spurn his kind mer - cy, Why will you long - er de - lay?
O - pen your heart, bid him wel - come, Save me dear Sav - ior I pray.

CHORUS.

What will you do, What will you do, "What will you now do with Je - sus?"

ff

Will you re - ject or take Him to-night, "What will you now do with Je - sus?"

No. 97.   What must it be to be There?

Geo. C. Stebbins. By per.

DUET.

1. We speak of the land of the blest, A coun-try so bright and so fair,
2. We speak of its pathways of gold, Its walls decked with jewels so rare,
3. We speak of its peace and its love, The robes which the glo-ri-fied wear,
4. We speak of its free-dom from sin, From sor-row, temp-ta-tion, and care,
5. Do Thou, Lord, 'midst pleasure or woe, For Heav-en our spir-its pre-pare,

And oft are its glo-ries con-fessed, But what must it be to be there?
Its won-ders and pleasures un-told, But what must it be to be there?
The songs of the bless-ed a-bove, But what must it be to be there?
From tri-als with-out and with-in, But what must it be to be there?
Then short-ly we al-so shall know, And feel what it is to be there.

REFRAIN.

To be there, to be there, Oh, what must it be

To be there, to be there,

to be there.   To be there, to be

to be there.   To be there,

there,   Oh, what must it be to be there?

to be there,   to be there?

By the Cross of Christ.

P. BILHORN.

ALFRED BEIRLY.

1. By the cross of Christ, our Sav - ior, We thro' faith are jus - ti - fied
2. By the cross we're lift - ed near - er To the heart of Him who died;
3. By the cross of Christ, our long - ings For a crown is sat - is - fied;
4. By the cross a fount of heal - ing Flowed from out His wound-ed side;

From all guilt and con - dem - na - tion, While we trust the cru - ci - fied.
Dai - ly grows our vis - ion clear - er To be - hold the cru - ci - fied.
Thoughts of joy be - yond are throng-ing As we stand the cross be - side.
Sin - ners, there in mer - cy kneel-ing, Seek ye now the cru - ci - fied.

CHORUS.

Allegretto. m

God for - bid that we should glo - ry Save in
God for bid that we should glo - ry

Je - sus' cross a - lone; For His blood still tells the
Save in Je - sus' cross a - lone; For His blood still

By the Cross.—Concluded.

sto - ry,   How for sin........   He did a - tone.

tells the sto - ry.   How for sin He did a - tone.

No. 99.   Autumn.

HENRY F. LYTE.   Spanish.

1. Je - sus I my cross have tak - en, All to leave and fol - low Thee,

FINE.

Na - ked, poor, de - spised, for - sak - en, Thou from hence my all shalt be.

D. S. Yet how rich is my con - di - tion, God and heav'n are still my own.

D S.

Per - ish ev - 'ry fond am - bi - tion, All I've sought, or hoped, or known,

2 Let the world despise and leave me,
    They have left my Savior too;
Human hearts and looks deceive me—
    Thou art not like them untrue;
Oh! while Thou dost smile upon me,
    God of wisdom, love, and might,
Foes may hate, and friends disown me,
    Show Thy face, and all is bright.

3 Haste then on from grace to glory,
    Armed by faith, and winged by prayer!
Heaven's eternal day's before thee,
    God's own hand shall guide thee there;
Soon shall close thy earthly mission,
    Soon shall pass thy earthly days,
Hope shall change to glad fruition,
    Faith to sight, and prayer to praise.

No. 100. I Come to Thee, Dear Savior.

P. B.　　　　　　　　　　　　　　　　　　　　　　　　　　P. Bilhorn.

1. I come to Thee, dear Sav - ior, Be - cause I need Thee so; I
2. I come to Thee, dear Sav - ior, My soul is sick of sin; I'll
3. I come to Thee, dear Sav - ior, To whom else can I flee, For
4. I look to Thee, dear Sav - ior, I see Thy wound - ed side; I

come, op-pressed in spir - it, O make me white as snow.
trust Thy blood to cleanse me, And make me pure with - in.
mer - cy, and for par - don? Oh let me hide in Thee.
see Thee bleed - ing for me, Thou Lamb once cru - ci - fied.

CHORUS.

I come, (I come,) I come, (I come,) Just now I come to Thee; (to Thee:) I

come to Thee, dear Sav - ior, Just now I come to Thee.

5 I see Thee resurrected,
　　From death to reign on high;
　I see Thee interceding,
　　To draw the sinner nigh.

6 I trust in Thee, dear Savior,
　　Thy blood now speaks for me,
　And as I bow before Thee,
　　Oh bid me live in Thee.

7 I rest in Thee, dear Savior,
　　My resting is complete;
　I find the sweetest comforts
　　While bowing at Thy feet.

8 Oh help me live, dear Savior,
　　Much fruit to bear in Thee;
　To glorify the Father
　　Through all eternity.

No. 101. Let it make thee Whole.

Frances R. Havergal.

P. Bilhorn.

1. Oh! the pre-cious blood of Je-sus, Shed on Cal-va-ry,
2. Pre-cious blood that hath redeemed us, All the price is paid!
3. Though thy sins are red like crimson, Deep in scar-let glow,
4. Pre-cious blood, by this we con-quer In the fierc-est fight;
5. Pre-cious, pre-cious blood of Je-sus, Ev-er flow-ing free!

Shed for reb-els, shed for sin-ners, Shed for you and me.
Per-fect par-don now is of-fered, Per-fect peace is made.
Je-sus' pre-cious blood can make them Whit-er than the snow.
Sin and Sa-tan o-ver-com-ing, Ev-er through its might.
Oh, be-lieve it, Oh, re-ceive it, Sin ner, 'tis for thee!

Chorus.

Oh! the pre-cious blood of Je-sus, Let it make thee whole,

Let it flow in might-y cleans-ing O'er thy sin-stain'd soul.

Copyright, 1886, by P. Bilhorn.

No. 102. Press toward the Mark.

El. Nathan.

James McGranahan.

1. Ring out the word from Christ the Lord, Our Cap-tain in the skies, To
2. He'll give the grace to win the race To him who brave-ly tries; For
3. Keep, then, the road: fight on for God, Though en-e-mies a-rise; The
4. Bear, then, the cross: count all things loss; On Je-sus fix your eyes; Till

all the saved who have believed: "Press toward the mark for the prize!"
Je-sus' sake the mes-sage take: "Press toward the mark for the prize!"
Lord with thee thy strength shall be: "Press toward the mark for the prize!"
Christ has come, till heav'n is won: "Press toward the mark for the prize!"

REFRAIN.

Press toward the mark for the prize! Press toward the

Press toward the mark for the prize! Press

mark for the prize! Let us suf-fer with Him and the

toward the mark for the prize!

"Well done" win, Press toward the mark for the prize!

No. 103. He Giveth Power to the Faint.

JULIA H. JOHNSTON.　　　　　　　　　　　　　　　　　　　　P. BILHORN.

1. Hast thou not known, hast thou not heard, That God, the Lord of all,
2. Lift up your eyes, be - hold on high, The ra-diant worlds a - far;
3. His word di - vine shall be thy guide, His love a sweet con-straint;

Who fail - eth not nor wea - ry grows, Up - hold - eth all that fall,
His word is pledged that none shall fail, He nam - eth ev - 'ry star.
O trust in Him who giv - eth grace And pow - er to the faint.

O sore - ly tried and troub-led heart, To Him bring thy com - plaint;
O doubt-ing heart, in faith draw nigh, The chil-dren's por - tion claim;
Wait, thou, on God, the Source, a - lone, Whence all thy com - fort springs;

Cres. — ff Rit pp - - - -

To wea - ry ones He giv - eth strength And pow'r un - to the faint.
He hath re-deemed from sin and death, He call - eth thee by name.
And thus thou shalt thy strength re - new, And mount on ea - gle's wings.

No. 104. Shall I be Saved To-night?

"Look unto me, and be ye saved."—Isaiah 45: 22.

FANNY J. CROSBY.   Mrs. M. BLISS WILSON.

1. Je - sus is plead-ing with my poor soul, Shall I be saved to-night?
2. Je - sus was nailed to the cross for me, Shall I be saved to-night?
3. Je - sus is knock-ing at my poor heart, Shall I be saved to-night?
4. What if that voice I should hear no more, Shall I be saved to-night?

If I be - lieve, He will make me whole, Shall I be saved to-night?
How can my heart so un - grate - ful be? Shall I be saved to-night?
What if His spir - it should now de - part? Shall I be saved to-night?
Quick - ly I'll o - pen this bolt - ed door, Save me; O Lord, to-night

Ten - der - ly, sad - ly I hear Him say, How can you grieve me from day to day?
Now He will save me by grace di - vine, Now, if I will, I may call Him mine;
O - ver and o - ver His voice I hear, Sweet - ly it falls on my list'ning ear;
Bless - ed Re - deemer, come in, come in, Pi - ty my sor - row, for - give my sin;

Shall I go on in the old, old way, Or shall I be saved to-night?
Can I the pleasures of earth re - sign? Oh, shall I be saved to-night?
Shall I re - ject Him—a friend so dear? Oh, shall I be saved to-night?
Now let Thy work in my soul be - gin, For I will be saved to-night.

By permission.

No. 105. Is it Well with your Soul?

P. H. ROBLIN.

P. BILHORN.

1. Is it well with your soul to-day, broth-er? With your
2. If the sum-mons of death should fall, broth-er? Should
3. If you still will re-fuse His love to choose, His
4. There's a prom-ise of life for you, broth-er, For

soul, your soul to-day? Are your sins all for-given of
fall, should fall to-day? Are you read-y to meet at the
love, His love to you, He may nev-er re-peat that
you, for you to-day, If you'll trust in the blood of the

CHORUS.

God in heaven? Is it well with your soul to-day? There's a
judg-ment seat, If the sum-mons should fall to-day?
call so sweet, Oh, then, broth-er, what will you do?
lamb of God, He will wash all your sins a-way.

foun-tain that's set for you, brother, A foun-tain of life for you. You may

wash and be clean from ev'-ry stain; Is it well with your soul to-day?

No. 106. There is Cleansing in the Blood.

W. A. WELLS.   Heb. 9:22. John 1:7. Eph. 1:7. Rev. 1:5.   P. BILHORN.

1. When the Sav-ior came to dwell be-low On the cross His won-drous
2. You have doubtless heard it oft be-fore Yet the Spir-it comes to
3. 'Twas for you the Lord was cru-ci-fied, See His bleed-ing hands, His
4. Hear and heed the Spir-it's plead-ing voice, Come! oh come, and make the
5. Sav-ior dear, to Thee my heart I bring, Now ac-cept my hum-ble

love to show, 'Twas that all this bless-ed truth might know There is
thee once more, And re-peats the sto-ry o'er and o'er There is
feet, his side, 'Twas for you he suf-fered thus and died, There is
Lord your choice, And this truth will make you to re-joice There is
of-fer-ing, That with all thy saved ones I may sing There is

CHORUS.

There is cleans - - ing   There is
cleans-ing in the blood, There is cleansing in the blood, in the blood, There is

cleans - - ing
cleansing in the blood, in the blood, All who in the Lord be-

There is Cleansing in the Blood.—Concluded.

lieve, shall have life, and joy, and peace, There is cleans-ing in the blood.

No. 107. Depth of Mercy.

God is Love. I John, 4: 8.

CHARLES WESLEY.   FROM STEVENSON.

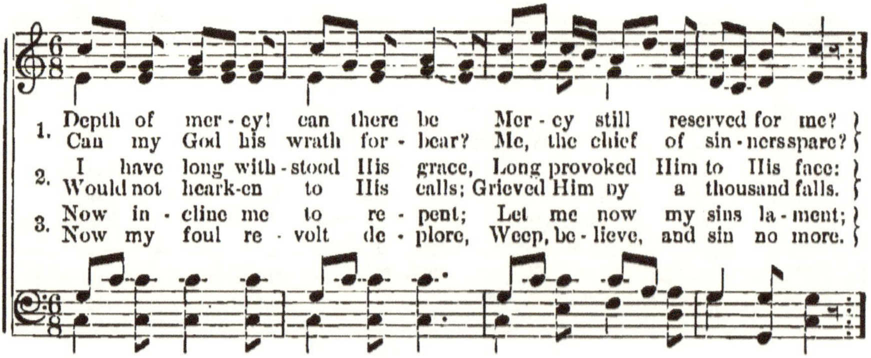

1. Depth of mer-cy! can there be   Mer-cy still reserved for me? }
   Can my God his wrath for-bear?   Me, the chief of sin-ners spare? }

2. I have long with-stood His grace, Long provoked Him to His face: }
   Would not heark-en to His calls;   Grieved Him by a thousand falls. }

3. Now in-cline me to re-pent;   Let me now my sins la-ment; }
   Now my foul re-volt de-plore,   Weep, be-lieve, and sin no more. }

CHORUS.

God is love! I know, I feel; Je-sus lives, and loves me still;

Je - sus lives, He lives and loves me still.

No. 108. A Happy Band are We.

P. B.

P. BILHORN.

1. We're a hap-py Chris-tian band, March-ing to the heav'n-ly land!
2. 'Tis a bright and cheer-ful way, When the Sav-iour we o-bey;
3. What a glo-rious morn 'twill be When our loved ones we shall see!
4. Come, and join us, one and all, Heed the Sav-ior's lov-ing call;

'Tis the Sav-iour leads us there To the Fath-er's home so fair!
By His lov-ing hand we're led, By His pre-cious man-na fed!
When with Je-sus we shall reign, Nev-er-more to part a-gain!
Turn from sin and seek the Lord, He will save you! Trust His word.

CHO. Come, and join . . . . our Chris-tian band, ... On re-

Come, and join our Chris-tian band, Chris-tian band,

demp-tion's ground we stand! We are ran-somed, we are

On redemption's ground we stand, ground we stand! We are ransomed, we are

rit. . . . . .

free, . . . Sing His praise . . . e-ter-nal-ly. . . . . .

free, we are free, Sing His praise e-ter-nal-ly, e-ter-nal-ly!

No. 109.   The King is Coming.

"Behold, I come quickly."—Rev. 22: 12.

RIAN A. DYKES.   IRA D. SANKEY. By per.

1. Re-joice! re-joice! our King is com-ing! And the time will not be long,
2. With joy we wait our King's re - turn-ing! From His heav'nly man - sions fair;
3. Oh, may we nev - er wea - ry watching, Nev - er lay our ar - mor down,

D. S. *joice! re - joice! our King is com-ing! And the time will not be long.*

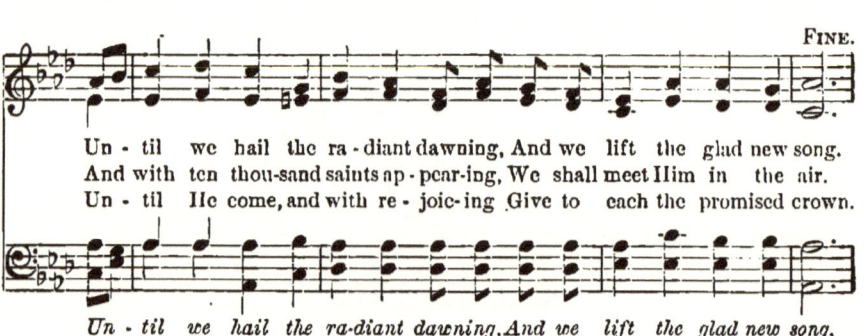

Un - til we hail the ra - diant dawning, And we lift the glad new song.
And with ten thou-sand saints ap - pear-ing, We shall meet Him in the air.
Un - til He come, and with re - joic-ing Give to each the promised crown.

Un - til we hail the ra-diant dawning, And we lift the glad new song.

CHORUS.

Oh, wondrous day! oh, glo-rious morn-ing, When the Son of Man shall come!

May we with lamps all trimm'd and burning Gladly welcome His re - turn! *Re-*

No. 110. Hallelujah! Look to Jesus.

"To give the light of the knowledge of the glory of God in the face of Jesus Christ."—2 Cor. iv. 6.

E. W. OAKES.　　　　　　　　　　　　　　　　　　　　　P. BILHORN.

1. Lift your eyes and look on Je - sus, See the glo - ries of His grace;
2. See the dis-tant hills of glo - ry Towering 'round the throne of God;
3. See the liv-ing wa-ters flow - ing, Flow - ing thro' the val - leys fair;
4. See Him in His life so low - ly, See Him on the cross of shame;

See the light and wondrous knowl-edge Of God's im - age in His face.
Hear the ran-som'd tell the sto - ry of the Sav - ior's pre-cious blood.
Thus the grace of God is show - ing Life to sin - ners ev - 'ry-where.
See Him Son of God most ho - ly, Glo - ry, glo - ry to His name.

CHORUS.

Hal - le - lu - jah! look to Je - sus, Hal - le - lu - jah! praise His name;

Hal - le - lu - jah! He will save you, Je - sus, ev - er-more the same.

No. 111. The Savior's Hand.

Peter Bilhorn. Geo. C. Stebbins.

1. The Sav - ior's hand is knock-ing, Is knock-ing at thy heart;
2. Hast thou not heard Him knock-ing, At morn-ing, noon and night?
3. The wound-ed hand of Je - sus, He of - fers now to thee;

O sin - ner bid Him wel - come, Lest grieved He should de - part.
A - rise, and bid Him en - ter, His pres - ence giv - eth light.
To save, to guide, to keep the Thro' all e - ter - ni - ty.

Chorus.

Knock - ing, knock - ing, knock ing, And long - ing to come in;

Oh! broth - er bid Him wel - come, He'll cleanse thy heart from sin.

No. 112. God be with You.*

"The grace of our Lord Jesus Christ be With you."—Rom. 16:20.

J. E. RANKIN. D. D. W. G TOMER. By Per.

1. God be with you till we meet a - gain,
2. God be with you till we meet a - gain,
3. God be with you till we meet a - gain,
4. God be with you till we meet a - gain,

By his coun-sels guide, up-hold you, With his sheep se-cure-ly
'Neath his wings se-cure-ly hide you, Dai-ly man-na still pro-
When life's per-ils thick con-found you, Put his arms un-fail-ing
Keep love's ban-ner float-ing o'er you, Smite death's threat'ning wave be-

fold you, God be with you till we meet a - gain.
vide you, God be with you till we meet a - gain.
round you, God be with you till we meet a - gain.
fore you, God be with you till we meet a - gain.

CHORUS.

Till we meet, till we meet, Till we
Till we meet, till we meet, till we meet, Till we

meet' at Je-sus feet, Till we meet, till we
meet at Je-sus' feet, Till we meet, Till we meet, till we

God be with You.—Concluded.

meet,   God   be   with   you   till   we   meet   a - gain.

meet,   till   we   meet,   God   be   with   you   till   we   meet   a - gain.

No. 113.   More Love to Thee, O Christ.

"Continue ye in my love."—John 15: 8.

Mrs. Elizabeth Prentiss.   Sir Arthur Sullivan. (1842.)

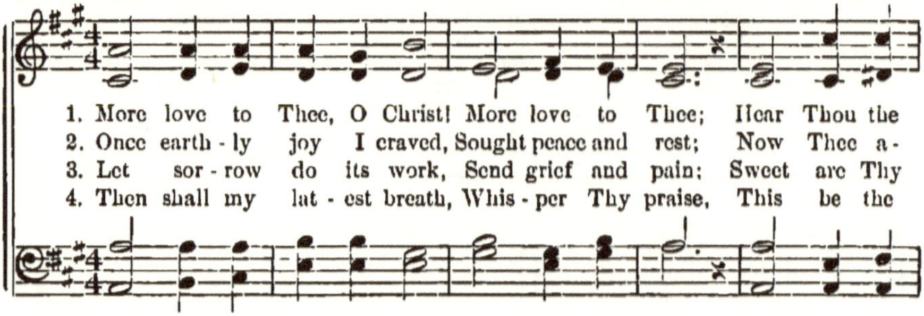

1. More love to Thee, O Christ! More love to Thee; Hear Thou the
2. Once earth - ly joy I craved, Sought peace and rest; Now Thee a -
3. Let sor - row do its work, Send grief and pain; Sweet are Thy
4. Then shall my lat - est breath, Whis - per Thy praise, This be the

prayer I make On bend - ed knee; This is my earn - est plea,
lone I seek, Give what is best; This all my prayer shall be,
mes - sen - gers, Sweet their re - frain, When they can sing with me,—
part - ing cry My heart shall raise; This still its prayer shall be:

More love, O Christ, to Thee, More love, O Christ, to Thee, More love to Thee!

Move Forward!

"The Lord is my light and my salvation.—Ps. 27: 1.

G. W. Crofts. D. B. Towner.

1. Move forward! valiant men and strong, Ye who have prayed and labored long, The
2. Move forward! each and ev'-ry one, The gold-en har-vest is be-gun, Ye
3. Move forward! reaping as you move! An-gels are watch-ing from a-bove! A-
4. Move forward! day will die full soon, How quick-ly eve-ning fol-lows noon, Now

time has come for you to rise, For lo! the sun rolls up the skies.
reap-ers, come from glen and glade And wield the sic-kle's glitt'ring blade.
round are wit-ness-es a host, A-rouse ye now and save the lost.
is the time to work and pray—Let glo-ry crown the dy-ing day.

Chorus.

Move for-ward, move for-ward, All a-long the line, Move

Move forward, move forward, All a-long the line, move for-ward,

for-ward, move for-ward, The light be-gins to shine.

move for-ward, move for-ward,

Thou art Drifting.

For Male Voices.

P. B.

P. Bilhorn.

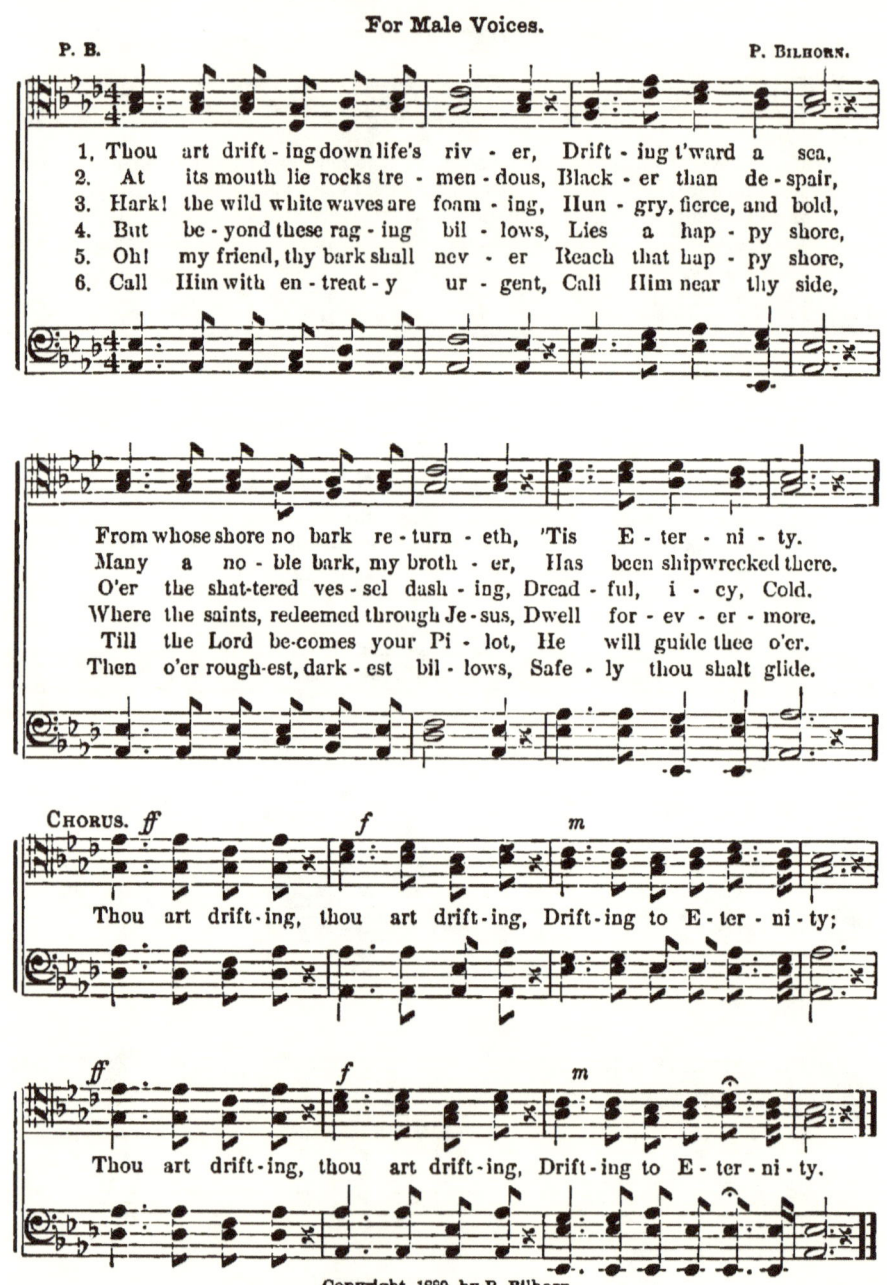

1. Thou art drift-ing down life's riv-er, Drift-ing t'ward a sea,
2. At its mouth lie rocks tre-men-dous, Black-er than de-spair,
3. Hark! the wild white waves are foam-ing, Hun-gry, fierce, and bold,
4. But be-yond these rag-ing bil-lows, Lies a hap-py shore,
5. Oh! my friend, thy bark shall nev-er Reach that hap-py shore,
6. Call Him with en-treat-y ur-gent, Call Him near thy side,

From whose shore no bark re-turn-eth, 'Tis E-ter-ni-ty.
Many a no-ble bark, my broth-er, Has been shipwrecked there.
O'er the shat-tered ves-sel dash-ing, Dread-ful, i-cy, Cold.
Where the saints, redeemed through Je-sus, Dwell for-ev-er-more.
Till the Lord be-comes your Pi-lot, He will guide thee o'er.
Then o'er rough-est, dark-est bil-lows, Safe-ly thou shalt glide.

Chorus. *ff*

Thou art drift-ing, thou art drift-ing, Drift-ing to E-ter-ni-ty;

Thou art drift-ing, thou art drift-ing, Drift-ing to E-ter-ni-ty.

No. 116. Tell it to Jesus.

J. E. RANKIN, D. D. Matt. xiv. 12. E. S. LORENZ.

1. Are you wea - ry, are you heav - y - heart - ed? Tell it to Je - sus,
2. Do the tears flow down your cheeks un - bid - den? Tell it to Je - sus,
3. Do you fear the gath'r - ing clouds of sor - row? Tell it to Je - sus,
4. Are you trou - bled at the thought of dy - ing? Tell it to Je - sus,

Tell it to Je - sus; Are you griev - ing o - ver joys de - part - ed?
Tell it to Je - sus; Have you sins that to man's eye are hid - den?
Tell it to Je - sus; Are you anx - ious what shall be to - mor - row?
Tell it to Je - sus; For Christ's com - ing King - dom are you sigh - ing?

CHORUS.

Tell it to Je - sus a - lone. Tell it to Je - sus, Tell it to Je - sus,

He is a friend that's well known; You have no oth - er

such a friend or broth - er, Tell it to Je - sus a - lone.

No. 117. In Everything Give Thanks.

Julia H. Johnston.   P. Bilhorn.

1. Give thanks in the night of thy sorrow, Rejoice in thy por-tion of pain,
2. Re-joice in a fin-ished sal-va-tion, A cov-e-nant or-dered and sure,
3. In all the fair days of clear shin-ing Look up to the source of thy light;
4. No e-vil can ev-er be-tide us, If God be our help and our shield,

There dawn-eth a bright-er to-mor-row, Thy loss shall bring in-fi-nite gain,
Oh! dread not the hour of temp-ta-tion, For "bless-ed are they that en-dure."
When com-forts and hopes are de-clin-ing, Re-joice in the strength of his might.
The Love that redeemed us, will guide us, And mer-cy shall still be re-vealed.

Chorus.

Give thanks un-to God and be joy-ful, What-ev-er may dai-ly be-fall,

Rejoice in the Lord, thy Redeem-er, Who rul-eth su-preme o-ver all.

No. 118. A Child of the King.

Miss JULIA H. JOHNSTON. P. BILHORN.

1. A child of the King! O call-ing di - vine! What rich-es of grace and
2. A child of the King! a child of the King! Then how can thy heart to
3. A child of the King! thy Fa-ther sup-plies, In wis-dom and love, thy
4. A roy - al de - gree, a child of the King! At last to his home, his

glo - ry are thine, Thy por - tion of all then joy - ful - ly claim, O
earth - li - ness cling? He calls thee his own, oh, mar - vel of love! Thy
wants as they rise, He know-eth thy way, he watch-es on high, No
own he will bring, Thy toil and thy care for - got - ten shall be, Made

CHORUS.

child of the King, he calls thee by name. A child of the King! be
life should be hid with the Fa-ther a - bove. A child, etc.
harm can be-fall, no e - vil come nigh. A child, etc.
like un - to him, his face thou shalt see. A child, etc.

joy - ful and sing, Be loy - al and lov-ing, Thou child of the King.

No. 119.

He Saves.

John 3: 17.

Frank M. Davis.

E. C. Avis.

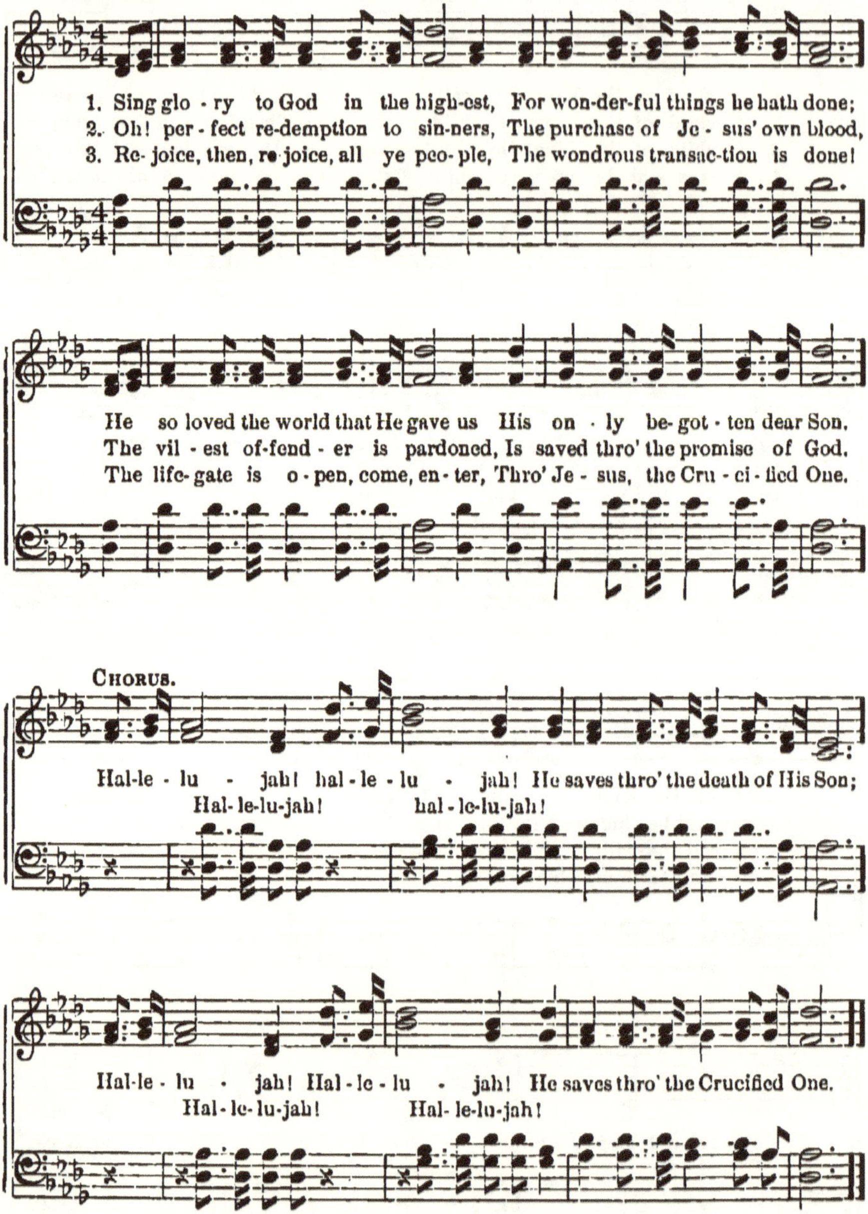

1. Sing glo - ry to God in the high-est, For won-der-ful things he hath done;
2. Oh! per - fect re-demption to sin-ners, The purchase of Je - sus' own blood,
3. Re- joice, then, re-joice, all ye peo-ple, The wondrous transac-tion is done!

He so loved the world that He gave us His on - ly be-got - ten dear Son.
The vil - est of-fend - er is pardoned, Is saved thro' the promise of God.
The life- gate is o - pen, come, en - ter, Thro' Je - sus, the Cru - ci - fied One.

CHORUS.

Hal-le - lu - jah! hal-le-lu - jah! He saves thro' the death of His Son;
Hal-le-lu-jah!   hal-le-lu-jah!

Hal-le - lu - jah! Hal-le-lu - jah! He saves thro' the Crucified One.
Hal-le-lu-jah!   Hal-le-lu-jah!

No. 120. Christ, my All.

HORATIUS BONAR, D. D. *"Christ is all, and in all."*—Col. 3:11. GEO. C. STEBBINS.

1. In the hour when guilt as-sails me, On His gra-cious name I call,
2. In the night when sor-row clouds me, And the burn-ing tear-drops fall,
3. In the day when this im-mor-tal Shall fling off its mor-tal thrall,
4. In the land of promised glo-ry, In the an-gel-crowded hall,

Then I find the heavenly fullness, Christ, my right-eous-ness, my all.
Then I sing the song of patience, Christ, my Broth-er and my all.
Then my song of res-ur-rec-tion Shall be Christ, my all in all.
This shall ev-er be my an-them—"Christ, my ev-er-last-ing all."

CHORUS.

All my song when standing yon-der, Shall be Christ, my joy, my all,

This shall ev-er be my an-them, "Christ my glo-ry, Christ my all."

Rit. _ _ _ _

This shall ev-er be my an-them, "Christ my glo-ry, Christ my all."

No. 121.   Jesus is Coming.

JESSIE E. STROUT.   MARK viii. 38.   P. BILHORN.

1. Lift up your voic-es, oh, loud let them ring, Je-sus is com-ing a - gain;
2. Ech - o it, hill-top! pro-claim it, ye plain! Je-sus is com-ing a - gain;
3. Sound it, old o-cean, in migh-ti - est wave! Je-sus is com-ing a - gain;
4. Soon we'll be wing-ing our flight thro' the air, Je-sus is com-ing a - gain;

Cheer up, ye pil-grims, be joy-ful and sing! For Je-sus is com-ing a - gain.
Com-ing in glo-ry, the lamb that was slain, For Je-sus is com-ing a - gain.
Tell to the islands and shores that ye lave, For Je-sus is com-ing a - gain.
Meet our be-lov-ed his glo-ry, to share, For Je-sus is com-ing a - gain.

CHORUS.

Je-sus is com-ing, is com-ing a-gain, Je-sus is com-ing a-gain, a-gain;

Com-ing in glo-ry for-ev-er to reign, Je-sus is com-ing a - gain.

No. 122. What a Gathering That will be.

J. H. K.

J. H. KURZENKNABE.

1. At the sound-ing of the trum - pet, when the
2. When the an - gel of the Lord pro - claims that
3. At the great and fi - nal judg - ment, when the
4. When the gold - en harps are sound - ing, and the

saints are gath - ered home, We shall greet each oth - er by the
time shall be no more, We shall gath - er, and the saved and
hid - den comes to light, When the Lord in all His glo - ry
an - gel bands pro - claim, In tri - umph - ant strains the glo - rious

crys - tal sea, With the friends and all the loved ones, there a-
ransom'd see, Then to meet a - gain to - geth - er, on the
we shall see; At the bid - ding of our Sav - ior, "Come, ye
ju - bi - lee; Then to meet and join to sing the song of

crystal sea,

wait - ing us to come, What a gath - 'ring of the faith - ful
bright ce - les - tial shore, What a gath - 'ring of the faith - ful
bless - ed to my right," What a gath - 'ring of the faith - ful
Mo - ses and the Lamb, What a gath - 'ring of the faith - ful

By Permission.

What a Gathering, etc.—Concluded.

CHORUS.

that will be!
that will be! What a gath - - - 'ring,
that will be! What a gath - 'ring of the loved ones when we'll
that will be!

gath - - 'ring, At the sound-ing of the glo-rious ju-bi-
meet with one an - oth-er,

lee! What a gath - - - 'ring,
ju - bi - lee! What a gath-'ring when the friends and all the

gath - - 'ring, What a gath-'ring of the faith-ful that will be!
dear ones meet each oth-er,

No. 123. He Knoweth Ye Have Need.

Matt. 6: 32.

Miss Julia H. Johnston.

P. Bilhorn.

1. O, soul in want and sor-row, The word of com-fort heed;
2. When far from God you wan-der In sin and doubt and fear,
3. In dark-ness and in dan-ger, His word of prom-ise plead,
4. He know-eth all your bur-den, The strife, and toil, and care;
5. When torn with pain and long-ing, Your hearts in an-guish bleed,

And trust your Heav'n-ly Fa-ther, Who know-eth ye have need.
He sees your need of par-don, He longs to bring you near.
O! flee to your Re-deem-er Who know-eth ye have need.
O! lay your wants on Je-sus, Who waits your load to bear.
The Com-fort-er is near you, He know-eth ye have need.

p CHORUS.

f

He know-eth ye have need, He know-eth ye have need,

cres. *p* *rit.*

In ten-der-ness He watch-es, He know-eth ye have need.

No. 124. When All the Saints Get Home.

Mrs. Harriet Jones.   D. B. Towner.

1. Oh, what a meet - ing that will be In that sweet time to come,
2. Oh, what a shout will fill the air When we the King be - hold,
3. Oh, how the up - per courts will ring When we our loved ones greet,
4. When close to Je - sus, the di - vine, We stand a - mong the throng,
5. The bat - tle o'er, the cross laid down, And safe a - cross the flood,

When we shall gain the vic - to - ry, And all the saints get home.
Who waits to bid us wel - come there With - in His bless ed fold.
In that bright home where an - gels sing, And all the ransomed meet.
Oh, what ec stat - ic bliss, to join In the re - demp - tion song.
With spot - less robes, and shin - ing crowns, All thro' the pre - cious blood.

CHORUS.

Home,   home,

Home, sweet home, blessed home, sweet home, The saints' e - ter - nal home,

home, sweet home,

Oh, what a meet - ing
Oh, what a hap - py meet - ing that will be, When all the saints get home.

By permission of D. B. Towner, owner of copyright.

No. 125. Trusting in the Promise.

Rev. H. B. Hartzler.

E. S. Lorenz.

1. { I have found re - pose for my wea - ry soul, }
   { And a har - bor safe when the bil - lows roll, } Trust-ing in the

2. { I will sing my song as the days go by, }
   { And re - joice in hope, while I live or die, } Trust-ing in the

3. { O the peace and joy of the life I live, }
   { O the strength and love on - ly God can give, } Trust-ing in the

promise of the Sav - ior; { I will fear no foe in the dead - ly strife, }
   { I will bear my lot in the toil of life, }

promise of the Sav - ior; { I can smile at grief, and a - bide in pain, }
   { And the loss of all shall be high - est gain, }

promise of the Sav - ior; { Who - so - ev - er will may be saved to - day, }
   { And be - gin to walk in the ho - ly way, }

REFRAIN.

Trust-ing in the prom-ise of the Sav - ior; Rest-ing on his

might - y arm for - ev - er, Nev - er from his lov - ing heart to

From "Songs of Refreshing," by per.

Trusting in the Promise. Concluded.

sev - er, I will rest by grace in his strong em - brace,

Trust - ing in the prom - ise of the Sav - ior.

No. 126. My Country, 'tis of Thee.

S. F. SMITH.   AMERICA.

1. My coun-try, 'tis of thee, Sweet land of lib - er-ty, Of thee I sing;
2. My na - tive coun-try, thee, Land of the no - ble free, Thy name I love;
3. Let mu - sic swell the breeze, And ring from all the trees Sweet free dom's song;

Land where my fa - thers died, Land of the Pil grim's pride, From ev' - ry
I love thy rocks and rills, Thy woods and tem - pled hills, My heart with
Let mor - tal tongues a-wake, Let all that breathe par-take Let rocks their

cres.

moun-tain side, Let free-dom ring.
rap ture thrills, Like that a - bove.
si-lence break, The sound pro - long.

4. Our father's God, to Thee,
Author of liberty,
To Thee we sing;
Long may our land be bright,
With freedom's holy light,
Protect us by Thy might,
Great God, our King!

No. 127. An All-Sufficient Savior.

"But my God shall supply all your need, according to his riches in glory by Christ Jesus."—Phil. 4: 19.

Words arr. by P. B.   P. BILHORN.

1. Art thou weak, af - flict - ed soul? I am strong to make thee whole;
2. Art thou faint-ing on the road? I am near to bear thy load;
3. Art thou much with grief op - prest? I am come to give you rest;

Art thou sick and hast no cure? I am thy Phy - si - cian sure.
Art thou hun - gry, thirs - ty, poor? I am rich to bless thy store.
Art thou wea - ry of thy sin? I am peace to thee with - in.

CHORUS.

I am read - y at thy side, At thy right and left to guide,

rit.

I am life, and love, and peace; I am joy which ne'er shall cease.

No. 128. Flee as a Bird.

MARY S. B. DANA. 1840.

Expression.

1. Flee as a bird to yon moun-tain, Thou who art wea-ry of sin;
2. He is the boun-ti-ful Giv-er, Now un-to Him draw near,
3. He will pro-tect thee for-ev-er, Wipe ev-'ry fall-ing tear;

Go to the clear flow-ing foun-tain, Where you may wash and be clean;
Peace then shall flow as a riv-er, Thou shalt be saved from thy fear.
He will for-sake thee, Oh, nev-er, Shel-tered so ten-der-ly there!

f Agitato.

Fly, for th'aveng-er is near thee, Call, and the Sav-ior will
Hark! 'tis thy Sav-ior call-ing, Haste, for the twi-light is
Haste, then, the hours are fly-ing, Spend not the mo-ments in

a Tempo.

hear thee, He on His bo-som will bear thee; Oh,
fall-ing, Flee for the night is ap-pall-ing, And
sigh-ing, Cease from your sor-row and cry-ing, The

rit.

thou who art wea-ry of sin, Oh, thou who art wea-ry of sin.
thou shalt be saved from thy fear. And thou shalt be saved from thy fear.
Sav-ior will wipe ev-'ry tear. The Sav-ior will wipe ev-'ry tear.

No. 129.　　　　　　**Seeking for Me.**

"For the Son of Man is come to seek and save that which was lost."—Luke 19: 10.

F. E. HASTY. By per.

1. Je - sus, my Sav - ior, to Beth - le - hem came, Born in a man - ger to
2. Je - sus, my Sav - ior, on Cal - va - ry's tree, Paid the great debt, and my
3. Je - sus, my Sav - ior, the same as of old, While I did wan - der a -
4. Je - sus, my Sav - ior, shall come from on high, Sweet is the prom - ise as

sor - row and shame; Oh! it was won - der - ful! blest be His name!
soul He set free; Oh! it was won - der - ful! how could it be?
far from the fold, Gen - tly and long He hath plead with my soul,
wea - ry years fly; Oh! I shall see Him de - scend - ing the sky,

REFRAIN.　　　　for me,............

Seek - ing for me, for me, Seek - ing for me, Seek - ing for me,
Dy - ing for me, for me, Dy - ing for me, Dy - ing for me,
Call - ing for me, for me, Call - ing for me, Call - ing for me,
Com - ing for me, for me, Com - ing for me, Com - ing for me,

for me,............

Seek - ing for me, Seek - ing for me, Oh! it was won - der - ful!
Dy - ing for me, Dy - ing for me, Oh! it was won - der - ful!
Call - ing for me, Call - ing for me, Gen - tly and long He hath
Com - ing for me, Com - ing for me, Oh, I shall see Him de -

Seeking for Me.—Concluded.

blest be His name! Seek - ing for me, for me.
how could it be? Dy - ing for me, for me.
plead with my soul, Call - ing for me, for me.
scend - ing the sky, Com - ing for me, for me.

No. 130. Touch and Cleanse Me.

MARY F. MARSH.　　　Matt. 8: 3.　　　WARREN W. BENTLEY.

1. Touch and cleanse me, bless-ed Sav - ior, I am wea - ry of my sin;
2. Touch and cleanse me, bless-ed Sav - ior, Hum-bly now my guilt I own;
3. Touch and cleanse me, bless-ed Sav - ior, I am poor, and weak, and blind;
4. Thou dost cleanse me, bless-ed Sav - ior, Light is stream-ing from a - bove:

I am long - ing for Thy fa - vor, Long-ing to be pure with - in.
Oh, be - stow Thy pard'ning fa - vor! Thou canst save me, Thou a - lone.
Grant me now Thy lov - ing fa - vor! Let me now sal - va - tion find.
Now I feel Thy pard'ning fa - vor! Oh, my soul is full of love.

D. S. *Touch and cleanse me, touch and cleanse me, Je - sus, save me or I die.*
D. S. *Thou dost cleanse me, Thou dost cleanse me, Glo - ry be to God on high.*

REFRAIN.　　　　　　　　　　　　　　　　　D.S.

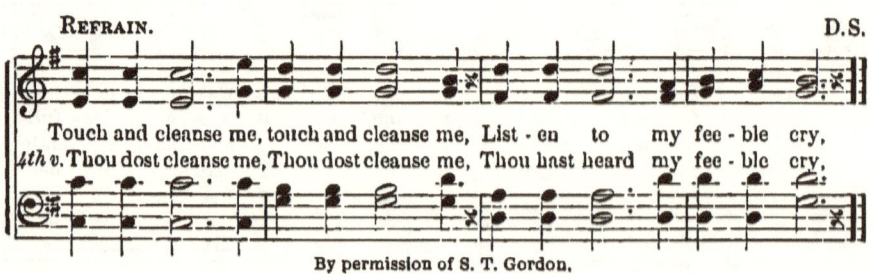

Touch and cleanse me, touch and cleanse me, List - en to my fee - ble cry,
4th v. Thou dost cleanse me, Thou dost cleanse me, Thou hast heard my fee - ble cry.

By permission of S. T. Gordon.

No. 131. Blessed Assurance.

F. J. CROSBY.   *" He is faithful that hath promised."—*Heb. 10: 23.   MRS. JOS. F. KNAPP.

1. Bless-ed as-sur-ance, Je-sus is mine! Oh, what a fore-taste of
2. Per-fect sub-mis-sion, per-fect de-light, Vis-ions of rap-ture
3. Per-fect sub-mis-sion, all is at rest, I in my Sav-ior am

glo-ry di-vine! Heir of sal-va-tion, pur-chase of God, Born of his
burst on my sight, An-gels de-scend-ing, bring from a-bove Ech-oes of
hap-py and blest, Watch-ing and waiting, look-ing a-bove, Filled with his

CHORUS.

Spir-it, washed in his blood.
mer-cy, whis-pers of love.   This is my sto-ry, this is my
good-ness, lost in his love.

song, Prais-ing my Sav-ior all the day long; This is my

sto-ry, this is my song, Prais-ing my Sav-ior all the day long.

No. 132. Seek The Lord and His Strength.

Miss Julia H. Johnston. Ps. 105:4. P Bilhorn.

1. Seek the Lord and His strength, seek His face ev-er-more, Turn to
2. There are fight-ings and fears both with-out and with-in, There are
3. Let not sin like a cloud, Hide the light of His face, O be-
4. O be lov-ing and loy-al, be faith-ful and true, For His

Him in the hour of your need; Sing to Him, "Sing His praise," talk of
foes on the left and the right, Take the ar-mor of God, put your
ware lest you stum-ble and fall, Do not share with an i-dol the
ban-ner a-bove you is Love; Look a-way from your self, from your

We shall con-quer and sing in the

Fine. **Chorus.**

all He hath done, He is might-y in word and in deed. "Seek the
trust in His name, And be strong in the power of His might.
love that He claims, Let the Sav-ior be all and in all.
weak-ness and fear, To Je-ho-vah who reign-eth a-bove.

name of the King, For the Lord is our strength and our song.

D. S.

Lord and His strength, seek His face evermore," We are weak but Je-ho-vah is strong;

No. 133. Saviour, Blessed Saviour.

GODFREY THRING.

HAYDN.

1. Sav-iour, bless-ed Sav-iour, Lis-ten whilst we sing, Hearts and voi-ces
2. Near-er, ev-er near-er, Christ, we draw to thee, Deep in ad-o-
3. Great and ev-er great-er Are thy mer-cies here; True and ev-er-

rais-ing Prais-es to our King, All we have, we of-fer;
ra-tion Bend-ing low the knee; Thou for our re-demp-tion
last-ing Are thy glo-ries there, Where no pain, or sor-row,

All we hope to be, Bod-y, soul, and spir-it,
Cam'st on earth to die; Thou, that we might fol-low,
Toil, or care is known, Where the an-gel le-gions

CHORUS.

All we yield to Thee.
Hast gone up on high. Sav-iour, bless-ed Sav-iour,
Cir-cle round thy throne.

Lis-ten whilst we sing, Hearts and voi-ces rais-ing Prais-es to our King.

No. 134. We Would See Jesus.

Miss Julia H. Johnston.

P. Bilhorn.

1. We would see Je - sus, Je - sus a - lone, He is the
2. We would see Je - sus, Spir - it of grace Teach us and
3. We would see Je - sus, Help - er and Guide, He will not
4. We would see Je - sus, He is the King, Oh! let us

Sav - ior, He can a - tone, All that we need, His grace will sup -
lead us, Show us His face, Now by Thy pow'r His Per - son re -
fail us, He will a - bide, We would see Him, in sor - row and
hast - en, trib - ute to bring, Now let us share His Cov - e - nant

CHORUS. Faster. ff

ply, While He is call - ing, O let us come nigh. We would see
veal, Oh, may we trust Him to par - don and heal.
joy, Still in His ser - vice the mo-ments em - ploy.
love, We shall be - hold Him, in beau - ty a - bove.

Je - sus, hear Him to - day, He is the Life, the Truth and the Way.

We would see Je-sus, Savior and friend, A - ble and will-ing to keep and de-fend.

No. 135. Hast Thou heard of Jesus?

Mrs. E. C. Ellsworth.　　　　　　　　　　　　　J. H. Tenny.

1. Hast thou heard of that won-der-ful Je-sus, Who
2. Hast thou heard of that won-der-ful Je-sus, Re-
3. Hast thou heard that this won-der-ful Je-sus, Dwells

dwelt a-mong sin-ners, a God? Who in pu-ri-ty walked with the
ject-ed by sin-ners of old? He is wait-ing to-day to be
now with the low-ly in heart? With the hum-ble he walks in com-

vil-est, Dis-pens-ing his fa-vors a-broad?
gra-cious, Yet slight-ed by num-bers un-told.
mun-ion; And grace he will free-ly im-part.

CHORUS.

Oh, that won-der-ful, won-der-ful Je-sus! He

left the bright glo-ry a-bove, On a world in its sin and its

Hast Thou heard of Jesus? Concluded.

ru - in, To pour out His in - fi nite love.

No. 136. Take my Life and let it Be.

FRANCES R. HAVERGALL.   HENDON.   C. H. A MALAN.

1. Take my life and let it be Con - se - cra - ted, Lord, to Thee;
2. Take my feet and let them be Swift and beau - ti - ful for Thee;
3. Take my lips and let them be Fill'd with mes - sa - ges from Thee;
4. Take my mo - ments and my days, Let them flow in end - less praise;

Take my hands and let them move At the im - pulse of Thy love,
Take my voice and let me sing Al - ways, on - ly, for my King,
Take my sil - ver and my gold, Not a mite would I with - hold,
Take my in - tel - lect and use Ev - 'ry pow'r as Thou shalt choose,

At the im - pulse of Thy love.
Al - ways, on - ly, for my King,
Not a mite would I with - hold.
Ev - 'ry pow'r as Thou shalt choose.

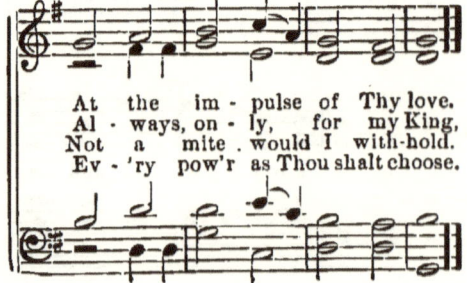

5 Take my will and make it thine,
It shall be no longer mine;
Take my heart, it is Thine own,
It shall be Thy royal Throne.

6 Take my love, my God, I pour
At Thy feet its treasure-store;
Take myself, and I will be
Ever, only. all for Thee.

No. 137. Ye Must be Born Again.

Verily, verily, I say unto thee, except a man be born again, he cannot see the kingdom of God.—John 3: 3.

Rev. W. T. Sleeper.

Geo. C. Stebbins.

1. A rul-er once came to Je-sus by night, To ask Him the way of sal-va-tion and light; The Master made an-swer in words true and plain, "Ye must be born a-gain, a-gain"
2. Ye chil-dren of men, at-tend to the word So sol-emn-ly ut-tered by Je-sus, the Lord, And let not this mes-sage to you be in vain, "Ye must be born a-gain, a-gain."
3. O ye who would en-ter the glo-ri-ous rest, And sing with the ran-som'd the song of the blest; The life ev-er-last-ing if ye would ob-tain, "Ye must be born a-gain, a-gain."
4. A dear one in heav-en thy heart yearns to see, At the beau-ti-ful gate may be watching for thee; Then list to the note of this sol-emn re-frain, "Ye must be born a-gain, a-gain."

a-gain..........

CHORUS.

a-gain, a-gain,

"Ye must be born a-gain, a-gain, Ye must be born a-gain, a-gain, I

Ye Must be Born Again.—Concluded.

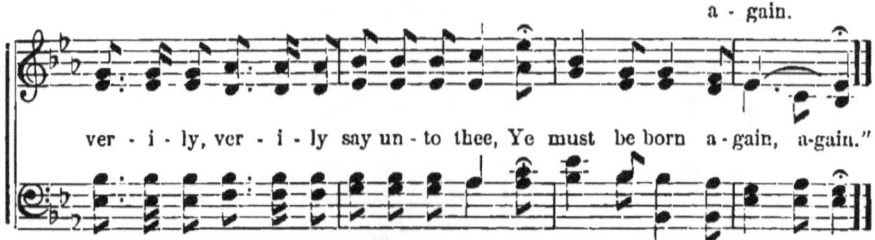

ver - i - ly, ver - i - ly say un - to thee, Ye must be born a - gain, a-gain."

No. 138. Must I Go, and Empty Handed?

After a month only of Christian life, nearly all of it upon a sick bed, a young man of nearly thirty years lay dying. Suddenly a look of sadness crossed his face, and to the query of a friend he exclaimed: "No, I am not afraid, Jesus saves me now; but oh, *must I go, and empty handed?*"

C. C. Luther.　　　　　Dan. 12: 3.　　　　　Geo. C. Stebbins.

DUET.

1. "Must I　go　and emp - ty hand - ed," Thus my　dear Re-deem - er meet?
2. Not at　death I　shrink nor fal - ter, For　my　Saviour saves me now;
3. Oh, the　years of　sin - ning wast - ed, Could I　but re - call them now,
4. Oh, ye　saints, a - rouse, be ear - nest, Up and work while yet 'tis day,

Not　one　day of　ser - vice give Him, Lay no　tro - phy at　His feet?
But　to　meet Him emp - ty hand - ed, Tho't of　that now clouds my brow.
I　would give them　to　my Saviour, To His will I'd glad - ly bow.
Ere　the　night of　death o'er-takes thee, Strive for souls while still you may.

CHORUS.

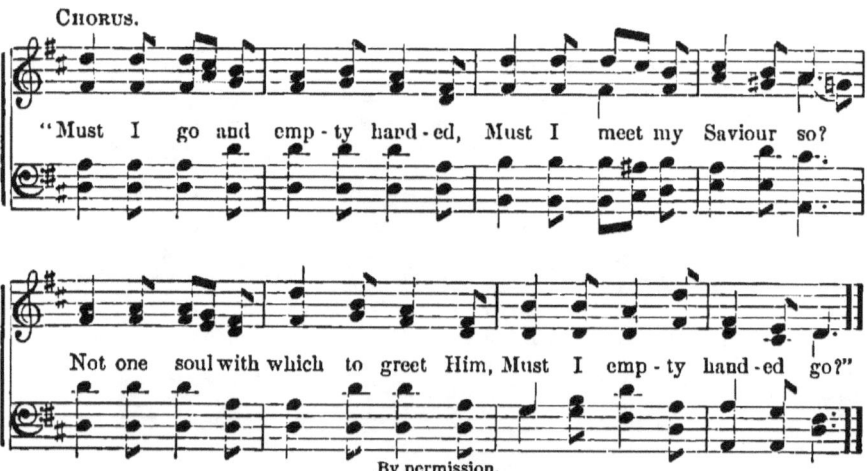

"Must I　go and emp - ty hand - ed, Must I　meet my Saviour so?

Not one　soul with which to greet Him, Must I　emp - ty hand - ed　go?"

By permission.

No. 139. I will Follow Thee, my Savior.

Dedicated to the Denver, Col., Y. M. C. A.

P. B.

PETER BILHORN.

1. I will fol-low Thee, my Sa-vior, Thou hast shed Thy blood for me; Lead me to the cleansing foun-tain, Where from sin I may be free.
2. I will fol-low Thee, my Sa-vior, Thou hast died to make me free; I am poor and weak and help-less, Therefore would I fol-low Thee.
3. I will fol-low Thee, my Sa-vior, All my dai-ly life shall be Con-se-cra-ted to Thy ser-vice, I will trust and fol-low Thee.
4. I will fol-low Thee, my Sa-vior, Tak-ing up my dai-ly Cross; Fol-low in Thy bleed-ing foot-prints, Counting earth-ly gains but loss.
5. As I fol-low Thee, my Sa-vior, Draw me near Thy wound-ed side, Till I reach the heavenly cit-y; Then with Thee be glo-ri-fied.

I will fol - - low, fol - - low,

CHORUS.

I will fol-low on-ly Thee, I will fol-low on-ly Thee, Yes! I'll

I will fol - - - low,

fol-low on-ly Thee, I will fol-low on-ly Thee, I will

I will Follow Thee.—Concluded.

fol - low on - ly Thee, Yes! I'll fol - low on - ly Thee.

No. 140.   While Jesus whispers.

"Come unto me, all ye that labor and are heavy laden."—Matt. 9: 28.

W. E. WITTER.   H. R. PALMER.

1. While Je - sus whis - pers to you, Come, sin - ner, come! While we are
2. Are you too heav - y la - den? Come, sin - ner, come! Je - sus will
3. Oh, hear his ten - der plead - ing, Come, sin - ner, come! Come and re-

pray - ing for you, Come, sin - ner, come! Now is the time to own Him,
bear your bur - den, Come, sin - ner, come! Je - sus will not de - ceive you,
ceive the bless - ing, Come, sin - ner, come! While Je - sus whispers to you,

Come, sin - ner, come! Now is the time to know Him, Come, sin - ner, come!
Come, sin - ner, come! Je - sus can now re - deem you, Come, sin - ner, come!
Come, sin - ner, come! While we are praying for you, Come, sin - ner, come!

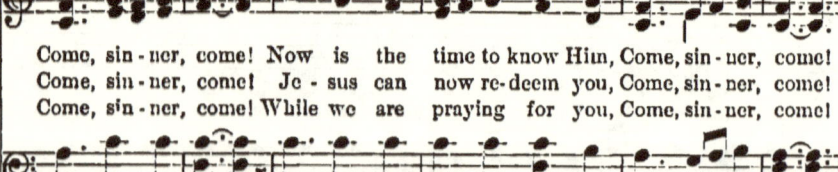

No. 141. Anywhere with Jesus.

"I will trust and not be afraid."—Isaiah 12: 2.

JESSIE H. BROWN.　　　　　　　　　　　　　　　　　　D. B. TOWNER.

1. An - y - where with Je - sus I can safe ly go, An - y - where He
2. An - y - where with Je - sus I am not a - lone, Oth - er friends may
3. An - y - where with Je - sus I can go to sleep, When the dark - ling

leads me in this world be - low. An - y - where with-out Him, dear - est
fail me, He is still my own. Tho' His hand may lead me o - ver
shad - ows round a - bout me creep. Know-ing I shall wak - en nev - er

joys would fade, An - y - where with Je - sus I am not a - fraid.
drear - est ways, An - y - where with Je - sus is a house of praise.
more to roam, An - y - where with Je - sus will be home, sweet home.

Chorus.

An - y - where! an - y - where! Fear I can - not know.

An - y - where with Je - sus I can safe - ly go.

No. 142. Blessed Jesus, Keep Me White.

P. B.   P. BILHORN.

1. Bless - ed Je - sus, Thou art mine, All I have is whol - ly Thine;
2. I am safe with - in the fold, All my cares on Thee are roll'd;
3. Pre - cious Je - sus, day by day, Keep me in the ho - ly way;

Thou dost dwell with - in my heart, Make me clean in ev - 'ry part.
I en - joy the sweet - est rest, For I'm lean - ing on Thy breast.
Keep my mind in per - fect peace, Ev - 'ry day my faith in - crease.

CHORUS.   white, ...

Bless - ed Je - - - sus, keep me white, keep me white, Keep me
     Bless - ed Je - sus,   keep me white,

walk - - - ing,

walk - ing, Keep me walk - ing in the light, . . . All I have . . . is
Keep me walk - ing   in the light,   All I have

whol - ly Thine, . . . Bless - ed Je - - sus, Thou art mine.
   is whol - ly Thine,   Bless - ed Je - sus,

Copyright, 1885, by P. BILHORN.

No. 143. Are You Coming While He Calls?

P. B.

P. Bilhorn.

1. You have heard the Gos-pel mes-sage, You have heard it o'er and o'er,
2. Is there one will now be-lieve Him, Is there one who'll turn from sin,
3. Will you give your self to Je-sus, Will you give your-self to God,
4. Are you com-ing? Are you com-ing? You have wan-dered far from God,

He that hear-eth and be-liev-eth Shall have life for-ev-er more;
Is there one will now re-ceive Him, And the heaven-ly life be-gin,
Will you trust His love and mer-cy, Will you trust His pre-cious blood?
There is par-don free-ly of-fered, There is cleans-ing in the blood?

Oh then why will you re-fuse Him, Oh then why will you de-lay
Is there one who knows his weakness, Is there one who knows his need?
Will you come un-to the foun-tain, Which for sin was o-pened wide,
Are you com-ing? Are you com-ing? Ere the judg-ment on you falls,

To be-lieve and trust in Je-sus, Who will wash your sins a-way?
Will you come while He is call-ing, Will you now the Spir-it heed?
Will you come while He is call-ing, Come un-to the Crim-son tide?
See the night is fast ap-pall-ing, Are you com-ing while He calls?

Are You Coming. Concluded.

CHORUS.

Are you com - ing, are you com - ing? There's a
Are you com ing, are you com - ing?

welcome and a par - don for you all, Are you com - ing
for you all, are you com-ing,

While He calls,............ Are you coming while the Sav - ior calls?
Are you coming while He calls,

rit.

No. 144. Softly Now the Light of Day.

G. W. DOANE.   GOTTSCHALK.

1. Soft - ly now the light of day Fades up - on our sight a - way;
2. Thou, whose all - per - vad - ing eye Naught es - capes, with - out, with - in,
3. Soon from us the light of day Shall for - ev - er pass a - way;

Free from care, from la - bor free, Lord, we would commune with thee.
Par - don each in - fir - mi - ty, O - pen fault, and se - cret sin.
Then, from sin and sor - row free, Take us, Lord, to dwell with thee.

No. 145. Rally Round the Cross.

The Battle Song of Victory.

E. F. M.   E. F. MILLER.

1. A-gain we have come in Je-ho-vah's name, The bat-tle to
2. When Is-rael of old marched a-round the wall, They blew with their
3. Our fa-thers, we know, to the Lord were true, They took up the
4. We all must en-gage if a crown we'd wear, And yon-der with
5. The con-flict will soon be for-ev-er o'er, The sum-mons will

fight and the vic-t'ry gain, We'll gird on the ar-mor and to the con-flict
trump-ets and shout-ed all; Then down came the walls, and they took the might-y
sword and they bat-tled thro'; They're safe now in glo-ry and look-ing down to-
Je-sus the glo-ry share; Then let all be true as we in-to bat-tle
come from the oth-er shore; And then home to glo-ry re-joic-ing we will

go, And in the name of Je-sus we'll con-quer ev-ery foe.
king; To God they gave the glo-ry, who did sal-va-tion bring.
night, They call to you and me to be faith-ful in the fight.
go, And res-cue ev-ery sin-ner from death and all its woe.
go, To praise him for the vic-tory he gave us here be-low.

CHORUS.

Then ral-ly! ral-ly! ral-ly round the cross! No one ev-er there will suf-fer

Rally Round the Cross.—Concluded.

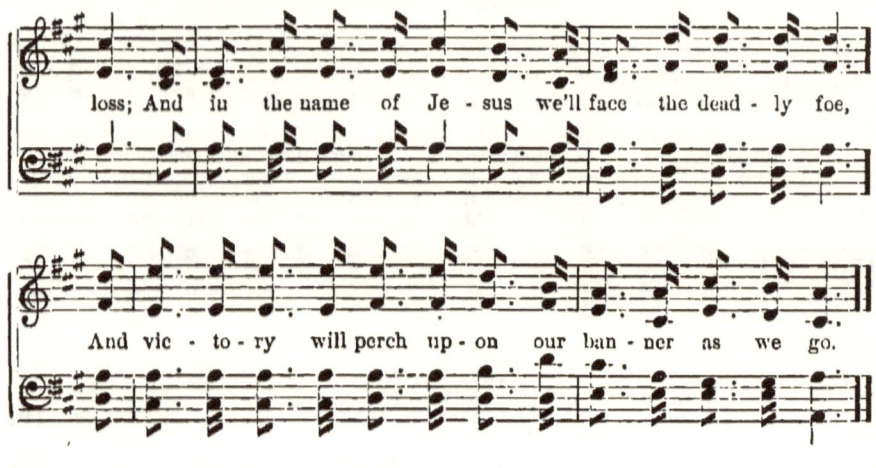

loss; And in the name of Je - sus we'll face the dead - ly foe,

And vic - to - ry will perch up - on our ban - ner as we go.

No. 146.   Belmont.

Rev. Samuel Stennett.   From Mozart.

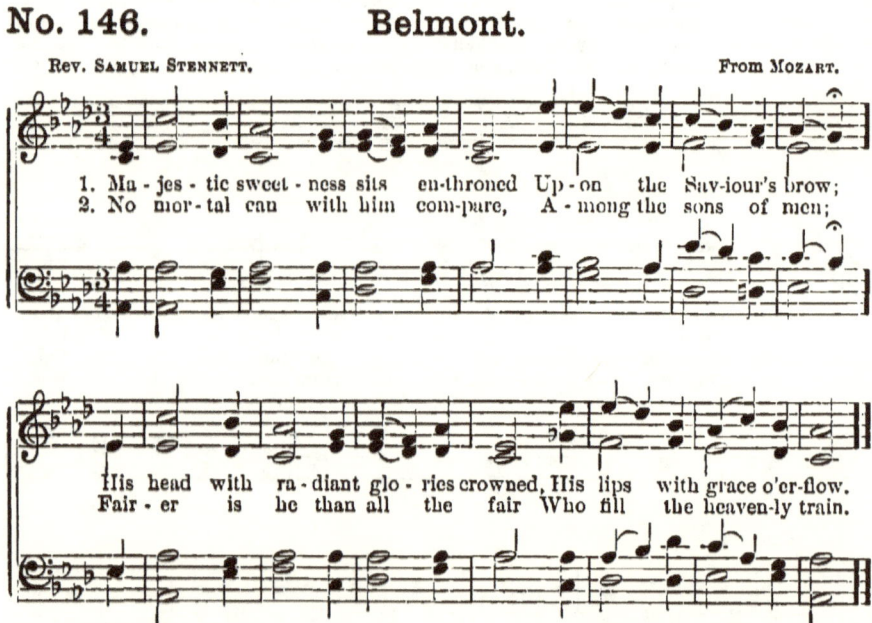

1. Ma - jes - tic sweet - ness sits en-throned Up - on the Sav-iour's brow;
2. No mor - tal can with him com-pare, A - mong the sons of men;

His head with ra - diant glo - ries crowned, His lips with grace o'er-flow.
Fair - er is he than all the fair Who fill the heaven-ly train.

3 He saw me plunged in deep distress,
  And flew to my relief;
For me he bore the shameful cross,
  And carried all my grief.

4 To heaven, the place of his abode,
  He brings my weary feet;

Shows me the glories of my God,
  And makes my joys complete.

5 Since from thy bounty I receive
  Such proofs of love divine,
Had I a thousand hearts to give,
  Lord! they should all be thine.

No. 147. Give Me Jesus.

FANNY J. CROSBY.   JNO. R. SWENEY.

1. Take the world, but give me Je - sus— All its joys are but a name;
2. Take the world, but give me Je - sus, Sweet-est com - fort of my soul;
3. Take the world, but give me Je - sus, Let me view his con-stant smile;
4. Take the world, but give me Je - sus; In His cross my trust shall be,

But His love a - bid - eth ev - er, Thro' e - ter - nal years the same.
With my Sav - ior watch-ing o'er me I can sing, tho' bil - lows roll.
Then thro'-out my pil - grim jour-ney Light will cheer me all the while.
Till, with clear - er, bright-er vis - ion, Face to face my Lord I see.

CHORUS.

Oh, the height and depth of mer - cy! Oh, the length and breadth of love!

Oh, the ful - ness of re - demp-tion, Pledge of end - less life a - bove!

By permission,

How Long?

JULIA H. JOHNSTON.　　　　　　　　　　　　　　　　P. BILHORN.

1. To-day the Redeemer is calling, He offers His
2. The world and its pleasures are pleading, The tempter is
3. Why linger in Satan's dominions? Your doubting and
4. How soon will you make the decision? O what will you
5. 'Tis Jesus the Lord and Redeemer Who asks you this

pardon and love, He's "able to keep you from falling" Presenting you faultless "above.
making his claim, But Jesus is now interceding, And longing to call you by name.
waiting are vain, Why halt you between two opinions, The Savior will keep and sustain.
gain by delay? Fear not to meet scorn and derision, Your life is fast passing away.
moment to choose, Be earnest, O trifler and dreamer! A kingdom and crown you may lose.

CHORUS. *Not too fast.*

How long will you keep Jesus waiting? To-day He commands you to choose, He offers a perfect Salvation, And you must accept or refuse.

No. 149. Holy, Holy! Lord God Almighty!

REGINALD HEBER. D. D.   Rev. 4: 8.   REV. JOHN B. DYKES.

1. Ho - ly, Ho - ly, Ho - ly! Lord God Al - migh - ty!
2. Ho - ly, Ho - ly, Ho - ly! all the saints a - dore Thee,
3. Ho - ly, Ho - ly, Ho - ly! tho' the dark - ness hide Thee,
4. Ho - ly, Ho - ly, Ho - ly! Lord God Al - migh - ty!

Ear - ly in the morn - ing our song shall rise to Thee;
Cast - ing down their gold-en crowns a - round the glass - y sea;
Though the eye of sin - ful man Thy glo - ry may not see,
All Thy works shall praise Thy name in earth, and sky, and sea;

Ho - ly, Ho - ly, Ho - ly! Mer - ci - ful and Migh - ty!
Cher - u - bim and Ser - a - phim fall - ing down be - fore Thee;
On - ly Thou art Ho - ly, there is none be - side Thee,
Ho - ly, Ho - ly, Ho - ly! Mer - ci - ful and Migh - ty!

God in three Per - sons, bless - ed Trin - i - ty!
Which wert and art, and ev - er - more shalt be.
Per - fect in pow'r, in love, and pu - ri - ty
God in three Per - sons, bless - ed Trin - i - ty! A - men.

No. 150. How can I live without Jesus.

Mrs. Emma Pitt.   Wm. J. Kirkpatrick.

1. How can I live without Je - sus? My Rock and my For-tress is he; I'm
2. How can I bear without Je - sus The storms that en - compass me here? For
3. How can I hope without Je - sus For He is my bright Morning star? His
4. How can I die without Je - sus? He'll be with me un - to the end; He

trust-ing a - lone in His mer - cy; He ev - er my Sav - ior will be.
tho' in the dark - est mid - o - cean, He speaks, "It is I, do not fear."
blood that hath bought my sal - va - tion, Brought me nigh who once was a - far.
nev - er will leave nor for - sake me, My lov - ing, un-change - a - ble Friend.

How can I live, how can I live, How can I live with-out Je - sus?
How can I live? how can I work? How can I bear with-out Je - sus?
How can I hope, how can I hope, How can I hope with-out Je - sus?
How can I die, how can I die, How can I die with-out Je - sus?

He is my Rock, He is my Hope! How can I live with-out Je - sus?
He is my Strength, Comfort and Song! How can I bear with out Je - sus?
His blood a - lone can guilt a - tone; How can I hope with-out Je - sus?
Je - sus, my Rock! Je - sus, my Hope! How can I die with-out Je - sus?

No. 151. Saved to the Uttermost.

W. J. K.

W. J. KIRKPATRICK.

1. Saved to the ut-ter-most: I am the Lord's; Je-sus, my Sav-ior, sal-
2. Saved to the ut-ter-most: Je-sus is near; Keep-ing me safe-ly, He
3. Saved to the ut-ter-most: this I can say, "Once all was dark-ness, but
4. Saved to the ut-ter-most: cheer-ful-ly sing Loud hal-le-lu-jahs to

va-tion af-fords; Gives me His Spir-it a wit-ness with-in,
cast-eth out fear; Trust-ing His prom-is-es, how I am blest;
now it is day; Beau-ti-ful vis-ions of glo-ry I see,
Je-sus, my King! Ransomed and par-doned, re-deemed by His blood,

REFRAIN.

Whis-p'ring of par-don, and sav-ing from sin. Saved, saved,
Lean-ing up-on Him, how sweet is my rest.
Je-sus in bright-ness re-vealed un-to me.
Cleansed from un-right-eous-ness, glo-ry to God.

Saved to the ut-ter-most: Saved, saved, by pow-er di-vine; Saved, saved, I'm

saved to the ut-ter-most: Je-sus, the Sav-ior, Is mine!

From "The Quartet," (Ark of praise), by per.

No. 152. Whiter than Snow.

" Wash me, and I shall be whiter than snow."—Ps. 51 : 7.

JAMES NICHOLSON.   WM. G. FISCHER. 1879, by per.

1. Lord Je - sus, I long to be per - fect - ly whole; I want Thee for -
2. Lord Je - sus, look down from Thy throne in the skies, And help me to
3. Lord Je - sus, for this I most hum - bly en - treat; I wait, bless - ed
4. Lord Je - sus, Thou seest I pa - tient - ly wait; Come now, and with -

ev - er, to live in my soul Break down ev - ery i - dol, cast
make a com - plete sac - ri - fice; I give up my - self, and what -
Lord, at Thy cru - ci - fied feet, By faith, for my cleansing, I
in me a new heart cre - ate; To those who have sought Thee, Thou

out ev - ery foe; Now wash me, and I shall be whit - er than snow.
ev - er I know, Now wash me, and I shall be whit - er than snow.
see Thy blood flow—Now wash me, and I shall be whit - er than snow.
nev - er said'st No, Now wash me, and I shall be whit - er than snow.

CHORUS.

Whit - er than snow, yes, whit - er than snow; Now

wash me, and I shall be whit - er than snow.

No. 153. "Come and See."

"Philip saith unto him, come and see."

W. A. O.　　　　　　　　　　　　　　　　　　　　W. A. Ogden.

1. 'Tis the gos-pel in-vi-ta-tion, 'Come and see, come and see,'
2. Oh, he nev-er will de-ceive you, 'Come and see, come and see,'
3. Come to Je-sus now con-fid-ing, 'Come and see, come and see,'

Un-to ev-'ry tribe and na-tion,'Come and see, come and see,'
Of your bur-den he'll re-lieve you,'Come and see, come and see,'
In His shad-ow quick-ly hid-ing,'Come and see, come and see,'

Je-sus of-fers free sal-va-tion, 'come and see,'
He is wait-ing to re-ceive you, 'come and see,'
In His mer-cy there a-bi-ding 'come and see,'

Chorus.

What the Lord hath done for me. Come and
What the Lord hath done for me.
What the Lord hath done for me.

see, (come and see,) come and see, (come and see,) What the

"Come and See."—Concluded.

Lord hath done for me, For He found my soul in sin, and He washed me pure and clean, This the Lord hath done for me.

No. 154. **Wilmot.**

C. M. Von Weber.

1. Lead me forth, O bless - ed Je - sus! Out of dark-ness, out of night,
2. Lead me forth, O bless - ed Je - sus! Leaving all my doubts and fears,
3. Lead me forth, O bless - ed Je - sus! In - to ful - ler, clear - er light,

In - to life and love e - ter - nal, In - to joy and in - to light.
Leav-ing all my sins and sor - rows, Leav-ing all my griefs and tears.
Where the sun - shine of thy pres - ence Falls up - on my in - ner sight.

4. Lead me higher still and higher,
   Draw me nearer, nearer thee;
   Touch my heart with love, and fit me,
   Lord, thy faithful child to be.

5. Lead me forth, O blessed Jesus!
   With a clear eye, fixed above,
   On the crown that now is waiting,
   In the Paradise of love.

No. 155. At the Feast of Belshazzar.

"And the king saw the part of the hand that wrote."—Daniel 5: 5.

KNOWLES SHAW.

KNOWLES SHAW.
Arr. by A. BEIRLY.

1. At the feast of Bel-shaz-zar and a thou-sand of his lords,
2. See the brave cap-tive, Dan-iel, as he stood be-fore the throng,
3. See the faith, zeal and cour-age, that would dare to do the right,
4. So our deeds are re-cord-ed, there's a Hand that's writ-ing now:

While they drank from gold-en ves-sels, as the Book of Truth re-cords,
And re-buked the haughty mon-arch for his might-y deeds of wrong;
Which the Spir-it gave to Dan-iel, this the se-cret of his might,
Sin-ner, give your heart to Je-sus, to His roy-al man-dates bow;

In the night, as they rev-elled in the roy-al pal-ace hall,
As he read out the writ-ing, 'twas the doom of one and all,
In his home in Ju-de-a, or a cap-tive in the hall,
For the day is ap-proach-ing, it must come to one and all,

They were seized with con-ster-na-tion, 'twas the Hand up-on the wall!
For the king-dom now was fin-ished, said the Hand up-on the wall!
Well he un-der-stood the writ-ing of his God up-on the wall!
When the sin-ners' con-dem-na-tion will be writ-ten on the wall!

At the Feast.—Concluded.

CHORUS.

'Tis the hand of God on the wall,
'Tis the hand of God that is writ-ing on the wall, 'Tis the

hand of God on the wall,
hand of God that is writ-ing on the wall, Shall the re-cord be "found wanting" Or

shall it be "found trusting," While the Hand is writ-ing on the wall?
writing on the wall.

No. 156. Lead me On.

C. C. CONVERSE. By per.

1. Trav-'ling to the bet-ter land, O'er the de-sert's scorch-ing sand,
2. When at Ma-rah, parched with heat, I the spark-ling fount-ain greet,
3. Thro' the wa-ter, thro' the fire, Nev-er let me fall or tire,

Fa-ther, let me grasp Thy hand, Lead me on, lead me on!
Make the bit-ter wa-ters sweet; Lead me on, lead me on!
Ev-'ry step brings Ca-naan nigher: Lead me on, lead me on!

4 When I stand on Jordan's brink,
Never let me fear or shrink;
Hold me, Father, lest I sink;
Lead me on!

5 When the victory is won,
And eternal life begun,
Up to glory lead me on!
Lead me on!

No. 157. Will the gates of Heaven be open?

E. R. LATTA.   C. E. LESLIE.

1. When my work is fin-ished! I'm try-ing to do, For my
2. When my toil-some jour-ney is end-ed be-low, And my
3. When the tears of sor-row, so com-mon to all, And each
4. Where no death nor sick-ness can ev-er-more come, And the

dear Re-deem-er, tho' hum-ble I be; Will the gold-en cit-y a-
feet, so wea-ry, for-ev-er are free, Will the walls of jas-per ef-
scene of trou-ble com-plet-ed shall be, Will the voice of Je-sus in
loved, if ho-ly, each oth-er shall see, Will I there be welcomed, no

rise to my view? Will the gates of heav-en be o-pen to me?
ful-gent-ly glow? Will the gates of heav-en be o-pen to me?
ten-der-ness call? Will the gates of heav-en be o-pen to me?
long-er to roam? Will the gates of heav-en be o-pen to me?

CHORUS.

O-pen to me, O-pen to me, Will the gates of heav-en be
Cho. for v 4. O-pen to me, O-pen to me, Yes the gates of heav-en will

By per.

Will the gates of Heaven.—Concluded.

o - pen to me, Will the gold - en cit - y a-
o - pen to me, Yes the gold - en cit - y will

rise to my view, Will the gates of heav - en be o - pen to me?
rise to my view, And the gates of heav - en will o - pen to me?

No. 158. Jesus Christ is Passing by.

"He heard that it was Jesus of Nazareth."—MARK. 10 : 47.

J. DENHAM SMITH.   MRS. JOS. F. KNAPP, by per.

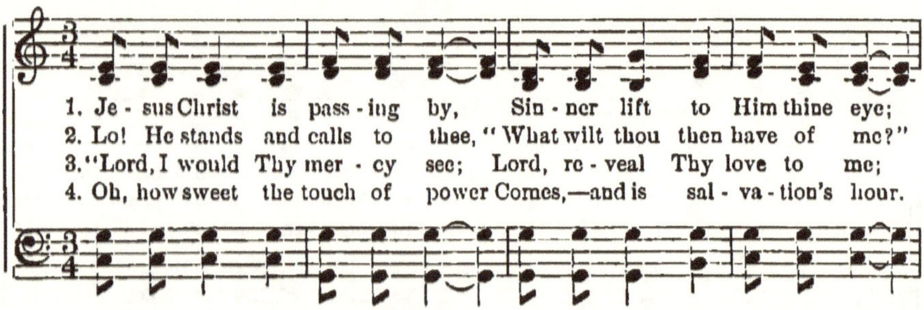

1. Je - sus Christ is pass - ing by, Sin - ner lift to Him thine eye;
2. Lo! He stands and calls to thee, "What wilt thou then have of me?"
3. "Lord, I would Thy mer - cy see; Lord, re - veal Thy love to me;
4. Oh, how sweet the touch of power Comes,—and is sal - va - tion's hour.

rit.

As the pre - cious mo-ments flee, Cry, be mer - ci - ful to me!
Rise, and tell Him all Thy need; Rise, He call - eth thee in - deed.
Let it pen - e - trate my soul, All my heart and life con - trol.
Je - sus gives from guilt re - lease, "Faith hath saved thee, go in peace!"

No. 159. Love, Rest, Peace and Joy.

P. B.

P. BILHORN.

1. There is love, true love, in the heav'n-ly home, Man-y
2. There is rest, sweet rest, in the home of God; 'Tis the
3. There is peace, sweet peace, in the home a-bove; For we'll
4. There is joy, glad joy, in the land of song, For in

dear ones there have gone, To be free from care, here no more to roam,
rest that Christ doth give, To the souls who trust in his pre-cious blood,
know no heart-breaks there; Sor-row ne'er shall come, 'tis a home of love,
heav'n we all shall sing; We are near-ing home soon to join the throng,

CHORUS.

There is love, there is

They have joined that hap-py throng.
They for-ev-er-more shall live.
Of that peace we all may share.
In the pres-ence of our King.

There is love,

rest, there is peace, there is joy,

there is rest, there is peace, there is joy, In that

land of song, where the loved have gone, There is love, rest, peace and joy.

No Night in Heaven.

Rev. 22: 5.

ALFRED BEIRLY.

1. No night shall be in heav-en; no gathering gloom Shall o'er that glorious
2. No night shall be in heav-en; no dread-ful hour Of men-tal dark-ness
3. No night shall be in heav-en, but end-less noon; No fast de-clin-ing

land-scape ev-er come; No tears shall fall in sad-ness
of the tempt-er's power; A-cross those skies no en-vious
sun, no wan-ing moon; But there the Lamb shall ev-er

o'er those flowers That breathe their fragrance thro' ce-les-tial bowers.
clouds shall roll, To dim the sun-light of the rap-tured soul.
shed His light. 'Mid past-ures green and wa-ters ev-er bright.

REFRAIN.

No night, no night shall be in heaven; No
No night, no night

Repeat pp.

night, no night shall be in heaven.
No night, no night

No. 161. Steer for the Light.

Mrs. Emma Pitt.   *"I am the Light."*—Jno. 8: 12.   James McGranahan.

Duet, if desired, to Chorus.

1. There's a beau-ti-ful light-house 'way o-ver the main, And the
2. O'er the beau-ti-ful riv-er with wa-ters so deep, Bright
3. See there from its height waves the ban-ner of love, All
4. For that ha-ven of rest, wea-ry sail-or, now steer, Or

bright beaming light you now see, 'Tis Je-sus, His love is now
an-gels are watch-ing the shore, The light-house stands firm and the
stud-ded with stars bright and free, And the ech-o comes, list! I've been
per-ish on life's storm-y sea, Fix your eyes on that light and His

point-ing the way, Come sail-or, He's wait-ing for thee.
storms nev-er sweep, For Je-sus has en-tered be-fore.
saved from the wreck By the light that's now beam-ing for thee.
voice you shall hear, "Come, sail-or, I'm wait-ing for thee.

Chorus.

Steer for the light, sail-or, steer for the light, To the
oar brave-ly bend and be bold; O steer for the light, sail-or,

Steer for the Light.—Concluded.

steer for the light, That beams from the shores of pure gold.

No. 162.   Only Trust Him.

J. H. S.

J. H. STOCKTON.

1. Come, ev - 'ry soul by sin oppressed, There's mer - cy with the Lord,
2. For Je - sus shed His pre - cious blood Rich bless - ings to be - stow;
3. Yes, Je - sus is the Truth, the Way, That leads you in - to rest;
4. Come, then, and join this ho - ly band, And on to glo - ry go,

And He will sure - ly give you rest, By trust - ing in His word.
Plunge now' in - to the crim - son flood That wash - es white as snow.
Be - lieve in Him with - out de - lay, And you are ful - ly blest.
To dwell in that ce - les - tial land, Where joys im - mor - tal flow.

CHORUS.

On - ly trust Him, on - ly trust Him, On - ly trust Him now;

He will save you, He will save you, He will save you now.

No. 163. Save Me, Lord.

ADDIE EVILSIZER.

L. M. EVILSIZER.

1. Lo! a poor and need-y sin-ner To the cross I cling,
2. There is per-fect peace and par-don For the sin-sick soul,
3. There's a house of man-y man-sions That is built on high,

Save me, Lord, save me, Lord! Noth-ing great have I to of-fer,
Praise the Lord, praise the Lord! Thro' the cleans-ing blood of Je-sus,
Praise the Lord, praise the Lord! Where His cho-sen shall be gath-ered

Nought but sin I bring, Save me, Lord, save me, Lord! Yes, I
Sin-ners are made whole, Praise the Lord, praise the Lord! "Come, and
To Him bye and bye, Praise the Lord, praise the Lord! Just a

know He died for sin-ners On Mount Cal-va-ry; And with
drink ye of the foun-tain, That is flow-ing free; Come, and
few more years of toil-ing For the Mas-ter here; Just a

Used by permission.

Save Me, Lord.—Concluded.

joy I hear his lov-ing voice, "I died for thee," I am com-ing,
low be-fore your Sav-ior hum-bly bow the knee. If you come be-
few more pray'rs to heav-en till the goal we near, Till he bids us

bless-ed Sav-ior, To Thy arms I fly, Save me, Lord, save me, Lord.
liev-ing, trust-ing, He will cleanse your soul, Praise the Lord, praise the Lord,
"Come up high-er," To that home a-bove, Praise the Lord, praise the Lord.

No. 164.   Only a Little While.

P. A. CROZIER.   GEO. C. STEBBINS.

1. On-ly a lit-tle while Of walk-ing with wea-ry feet,
2. Suf-fer if God shall will, And work for Him while we may, From
3. On-ly a lit-tle while For toil-ing a few short days, And

Pa-tient-ly o-ver the thorn-y way That leads to the gold-en street.
Cal-va-ry's cross to Zi-on's crown, Is on-ly a lit-tle way.
then comes the rest, the qui-et rest, E-ter-ni-ty's end-less praise.

No. 165. I long to know Thee better.

" Whom to know aright is life eternal."

Mrs. M. L. Davidson, J. H. Fillmore.

1. I long to know Thee bet-ter, To un-der-stand Thy will,
2. O Sav-ior, draw me near-er, There's safe-ty at Thy side.
3. With Thee the des-ert drea-ry Is robbed of all its gloom,

That I may loose the fet-ter, That keeps me from Thee still.
And there Thy love is dear-er, Than all the world be-side.
The way so long and wea-ry Like sum-mer gar-dens bloom.

CHORUS.

I long to know Thee bet-ter, To un-der-stand Thy will,

My Sav-ior and my help-er, Thy love in me ful-fil.

By permission.

No. 166. Will You Come?

C. E. L.

C. E. LESLIE.

Allegro.

1. Will you come one and all to the Lamb that was slain?
2. There's a work to be done, there's a cross you should bear,
3. You have friends who have gone to that ha-ven of rest,

Will you come to his arms and be cleansed from all stain,
There's a crown to be won, there's a crown you should wear,
Whom you prom-ised to meet in the land of the blest,

He in-vites you to-day, Do not then stay a-way.
He in-vites you to-day, Do not then stay a-way.
Do not then stay a-way, He in-vites you to-day.

CHORUS.

Bless-ed be the Lord, he in-vites you to-day, Bless-ed be the Lord,

Bless-ed be the Lord, Bless-ed be the Lord, he in-vites you to day.

By permission.

No. 167. Church Rallying Song.

FANNY J. CROSBY.   JOHN R. SWENEY.

1. A-wake! a-wake! the Mas-ter now is call-ing us, A-rise! a-rise! and, trust-ing in his word, Go forth, go forth! pro-claim the year of ju-bi-lee, And take the cross, the bless-ed cross of Christ our Lord.

2. A cry for light from dy-ing ones in hea-then lands; It comes, it comes a-cross the o-cean's foam; Then haste, oh, haste to spread the words of truth a-broad, For-get-ting not the starv-ing poor at home, dear home.

3. O church of God, ex-tend thy kind, ma-ter-nal arms To save the lost on mountains dark and cold, Reach out thy hand with lov-ing smile to res-cue them, And bring them to the shel-ter of the Sav-ior's fold.

4. Look up! look up! the prom-ised day is draw-ing near, When all shall hail, shall hail the Sav-ior King, When peace and joy shall fold their wings in ev-'ry clime, And "glo-ry, hal-le-lu-jah," o'er the earth shall ring.

CHORUS.

On, on, swell the cho-rus;

On, on, on, swell the cho-rus,

Church Rallying Song.—Concluded.

On, on, the morn-ing star is shin-ing o'er us; On, on, while be-
On, on, on,

fore us Our might-y, might-y Sav-ior leads the way;
while be-fore leads the way:

{ Glo - ry, glo - ry, hear the ev - er - last - ing throng, }
{ Shout ho - san - na, while we bold - ly march a - long; }

Faith - ful sol - diers here be - low, On - ly Je - sus will we know,

Shout - ing "free sal - va - tion" o'er the world we go.

No. 168. The Master's Call.

" Go, work to-day in my vine-yard."—MATT. xxi. 28.

JULIA STERLING.   IRA D. SANKEY. By per.

1. Be-hold, the Mas-ter now is call-ing For reap-ers brave and true;
2. Go forth, and res-cue those that per-ish, Where sin and dark-ness reign;
3. Go, bid the poor with joy and glad-ness The feast of love to share;
4. Go forth, the sum-mer days are wan-ing, Their light will soon be o'er;

The gold-en har-vest fields are wait-ing, But la-bour-ers are few.
Go, lend a help-ing hand to save them, And break the tempt-er's chain.
And He the Bread of Life E-ter-nal Will make them wel-come there.
The sol-emn hour is quick-ly com-ing, When we can work no more.

CHORUS.

Go forth, with pa-tience, love and kind-ness; And in the Mas-ter's name,

The bless-ed news of free sal-va-tion To all the world pro-claim.

Copyright 1887, by Ira D. Sankey.

No. 169. Wait, and Murmur Not.

"It is good that a man hope and quietly wait."—Sam. 3: 26

W. H. Bellamy.

Wm. J. Kirkpatrick.

1. O troubled heart, there is a home, Be-yond the reach of toil and care;
2. Yet when bow'd down beneath the load By heav'n al-lowed, thine earthly lot;
3. If in thy path some thorns are found, O, think who wore them on His brow;
4. Toil on, nor deem, tho' sore it be, One sigh un-heard, one pray'r for-got;

A home where chang-es nev - er come, Who would not fain be rest - ing there?
Look up! thou'lt reach that sweet a - bode, Wait, meek-ly wait, and murmur not.
If grief thy sorrowing heart has found, It reached one ho - li - er than thou.
The day of rest will dawn for thee; Wait, meek-ly wait, and murmur not.

Chorus.

O, wait, meek - ly wait, and mur - mur not, O
meek - ly wait,

wait, meek - ly wait, and mur-mur not; O, wait, meek - ly wait,
meek - ly wait,

O, wait, O, wait, and mur - mur not.
meek - ly wait, O, murmur not.

By permission.

No. 170. A Bright To-Morrow.

F. H. Jacobs. Alfred Beirly.

1. If aught of thy life should be sav-ored with sor-row,
2. Should ev-er the weight of a sad thought per-plex thee;
3. Go gath-er the sun-shine and scat-ter it sweet-ly;

Or part of thy path-way o'er-shad-owed with gloom,
Or wak-en a chord that sounds harsh to thine ear,
Where need-ed as-sis-tance is ev-er made known,

Then be not dis-mayed, 'twill be bet-ter to-mor-row,
Then whis-per a pray'r, for thy Sav-ior will hear thee;
Be one of the few who in life's course com-plete-ly

When the sun shall break forth in the splen-dor of noon,
And mark the sweet chime in the fall of a tear,
Are lost to them-selves, but their Sav-ior en-throne,

CHORUS.
Then to Je-sus draw near, ... Ev-er be of good

Then to Je-sus draw near,

Copyright. 1889, by P. Bilhorn.

A Bright To-Morrow—Concluded.

Ev - er be of good cheer; Then to Je - sus draw near, Ev - er

be of good cheer, He knows all thy sor - row, And thy pray'r he will hear.

No. 171. And Can I Yet Delay?

Dr. L. Mason.

1. And can I yet de - lay My lit - tle all to give?
2. Nay, but I yield, I yield! I can hold out no more;
3. Tho' late, I all for - sake,— My friends, my all re - sign;
4. Come, and pos - sess me whole, Nor hence a - gain re - move;

To tear my soul from earth a - way, For Je - sus to re - ceive?
I sink, by dy - ing love compell'd, And own thee con - quer - or!
Gra - cious Re - deem - er, take, oh! take And seal me ev - er thine.
Set - tle and fix my wav'ring soul With all thy weight of love.

No. 172.

Look unto Me.

"Look unto Me, and be ye saved."—Isiah 14: 22.

W. P. MACKAY.   IRA D. SANKEY. By per.

1. "Look un-to Me, and be ye saved!" Look, men of na-tions all;
2. "Look un-to Me, and be ye saved!" Look now, nor dare de-lay;
3. "Look un-to Me, and be ye saved!" Look from your doubts and fears;
4. "Look un-to Me, and be ye saved!" Look to the work all done;

Look, rich and poor; look, old and young; Look, sin-ners, great and small!
Look as you are,—lost, guilt-y, dead; Look while 'tis called to-day.
Look from your sins of crim-son dye, Look from your prayers and tears.
Look to the pierc-ed Son of Man; Look, and your sins are gone!

REFRAIN.

Look un-to Him, and be ye saved! O wea-ry, trou-bled soul;

Oh, look to Je-sus while you may: One look will make thee whole!

No. 173.   Who Can it Be?

W. A. O.

W. A. OGDEN, by per.

1. I've wan-dered in sor-row and sin, My heart it was heav-y and
2. I've strug-gled in doubt and in fear, Not know-ing to whom I should
3. I've heard it a-gain and a-gain, Wher-ev-er my foot-steps did
4. I turned to my Fa-ther a-bove, I read of his prom-is-es
5. I'm grop-ing in dark-ness no more, His glo-ry il-lu-mines my

sore, I heard a voice say-ing, "A-rise and come in, And
go, I heard a voice say-ing, "Son, be of good cheer," So
roam, It melt-ed my heart with its pit-y-ing strain, It
sure, I thought of my Sav-ior, His cross and His love, And
way; I'm walk-ing by faith, and His prom-is-es are My

REFRAIN.

wan-der in sor-row no more. Who can it be? Who can it be?
sooth-ing-ly ten-der and low. Who can it be? Who can it be?
light-ed my soul of its gloom. Oh, it was Thee! Oh, it was Thee!
oh! what a Friend I found there! Oh, what a Friend! Oh, what a Friend!
sol-ace and joy ev-'ry day. Yes, ev-'ry day! Yes, ev-'ry day!

rit.   *ad lib.*

Thus I was won-der-ing, Who can it be, Ten-der-ly call-ing to me?
Thus I was won-der-ing, Who can it be, Ten-der-ly call-ing to me?
Sav-ior of men, O my Je-sus, 'twas Thee! Ten-der-ly call-ing to me?
Sav-ior from sin thou hast been un-to me, Sav-ior from sin un-to me.
Je-sus of Naz-a-reth light-eth my way, Je-sus now light-eth my way.

By permission.

No. 174.   Oh List to the Call!

LAURA E. NEWELL.   C. E. LESLIE.

1. Oh list to the call, He is yearning for thee, O - bey Him, and from
2. Oh list to the call, He is pleading for you, His love will pre - vail,
3. Oh list to the call, and in Je - sus con - fide, In faith, love and hope

all thy bur - dens be free; He knows of thy cares, and His
and His prom-ise is true; He stands at the gate, there to
ev - er walk by His side; Cling close to the Sav - ior, He'll

in - fi - nite love Will ten - der - ly lead thee to
wel - come us all, Oh list to His plead - ing, oh
nev - er for - sake, For all who will trust Him His

CHORUS.

man - sions a - bove.
list to the call.   He is plead - ing for all;
love shall par-take.   Oh list to the call,..........   The

Then why should we fear, Oh list to His call, for the
Sav - ior is near,.......

By permission.

Oh List, etc.—Concluded.

Sav - ior is near, He glad - ly would heal thee, thy soul He will cheer.

No. 175. Come, Ye Sinners, Poor and Needy.

1. Come, ye sin - ners, poor and need-y, Weak and wounded, sick and sore,
2. Ho, ye need - y; come, and welcome; God's free boun - ty glo - ri - fy!
3. Let not conscience make you lin - ger, Nor of fit - ness fond-ly dream;

Je - sus read - y stands to save you, Full of pi - ty, love, and power,
True be - lief and true re - pent-ance, Ev - ery grace that brings us nigh,
All the fit - ness he re - quir-eth Is to feel your need of him;

He is a - ble, He is a - ble, He is will - ing, doubt no more.
With - out mon - ey, With - out money, Come to Je - sus Christ, and buy.
This he gives you; This he gives you; 'Tis the Spir - it's ris - ing beam.

No. 176. Salvation! O Sing the Story.

P. BILHORN. ALFRED BEIRLY.

1. Sal - va - tion! O sing the glad sto - ry, Sal - va - tion to sin-ners make known;
2. Sal - va - tion! O, sin-ners, re-ceive it, Ac - cept the glad mes-sage of God;
3. Now free-ly God of - fers sal - va - tion, Full par-don and pu - ri - ty true;
4. O trust in the mer - cy He of - fers, And cleave to the path He hath trod;

For Je - sus, descending from glo - ry, A ran-som be-came for His own.
Take now the full par-don He of - fers, And trust in the sin-cleansing blood.
Re - ceive it with glad ac-cla - ma - tion, Let Christ be a Sav - ior to you.
And you shall re-joice in sal - va - tion, Re-joice in your Sav - ior and God.

CHORUS.

Sal - va - tion, sal - va - tion.

Sal-va-tion He of-fers, sal-va-tion He of-fers, Proclaim of the sin-cleansing blood;

Sal - va - tion, sal - va - tion.

Sal - va-tion He of-fers, sal-va-tion He of-fers, Ring out the sweet message of God.

Used by per. Copyright, 1889, by A. Beirly.

No. 177. Sweet Surprises.

T. T. BACHELLER.

NORMAN M. MATTICE.

1. Sweet sup - pris - es wait the chris - tian, In the fa - thers home on high;
2. Loft - iest flights of hu - man fan - cy, Can - not grasp a sin - gle trace;
3. Bright - er than the pierc-ing sun - rays, Clear - er than the moon's pure light,

Mu - sic, earth - ly ear hath heard not, Scenes, too bright for mor - tal eye.
Of the heav'n per-vad - ing glo - ry, Beam-ing from the Sav - ior's face.
Is the glo - ry, grand, e - ter - nal, Of that land that knows no night.

CHORUS.

Let us hear the Spir - it, whisp'ring Of the heav'n - ly joys, to come;

Rit.

Live by faith in him who saved us, Till we reach that glorious home.

No. 178. There awaits a Crown.

NEVA E. PARKHILL.

C. E. LESLIE.

1. I will try to be a sol-dier of the cross,
2. I will try to be a sol-dier of the cross,
3. I will try to be a sol-dier of the cross, (of the cross,)

Tho' its ban - ner leads in wild and rug - ged ways;
For my Sav - ior keep - eth watch and ward a - bove;
And the spir - it will not sink be - neath its load;

Tho' the spir - it meets with bur - den and with loss, (and with loss,)
He will make the spir - it tri - umph o - ver loss, (o - ver loss,)
For the dear - est ties of earth are on - ly dross, (on - ly dross,)

And the clouds of grief may shad - ow all my days.
For He lead - eth all His chil - dren in His love.
And our souls should on - ly up - ward look to God.

By per.

There awaits a Crown.—Concluded.

On - ward, sol - - - dier, to the bat - - - tle,

On - ward, sol - dier, on, to the bat - tle, on,

Ther a - waits a crown of beau - ty and of light,

Gird thine arm - - - - or, be thy ar - - - - dor,

Gird thine arm - or on, be thy ar - dor stroug,

To the bat - tle in his glo - ry and might.

No. 179. Do the Right.

Rev. N. McLead. P. Bilhorn.

1. Courage broth-er, do not stum-ble, Tho' thy path be dark as night,
2. If the road be rough and drear-y, And its end far out of sight,
3. Sim-ple rule, and saf-est guid-ing, In-ward peace, and in-ward might,
4. Some will hate and some will love thee, Some will flatt-er, some will slight,

There's a hand to guide the hum-ble, Trust in God and do the right.
Tread it brave-ly, strong or wea-ry, Trust in God and do the right.
Comes while in his love a-bid-ing, Trust-ing God and do-ing right.
Heed them not but look a-bout thee, Trust in God and do the right

CHORUS.

Do the right, do the right,

Do the right, do the right, Trust in God and do the right, (do the right,)

Courage broth-er do not stum-ble, Trust in God and do the right.

No. 180. Bringing in the Sheaves.

Words from "Songs of Glory." Geo. A. Minor, by per.

1. Sow - ing in the morn - ing, sow - ing seeds of kind - ness,
2. Sow - ing in the sun - shine, sow - ing in the shad - ows,
3. Go, then, ev - er weep - ing, sow - ing for the Mas - ter,

Sow-ing in the noon-tide, and the dew-y eves; Wait-ing for the har-vest,
Fear-ing nei-ther clouds nor winter's chilling breeze; By and by the har-vest,
Tho' the loss sus-tain'd our spir-it of-ten grieves; When our weeping's o - ver,

and the time of reap - ing, We shall come re - joic - ing,
and the la - bor end - ed, We shall come re - joic - ing,
He will bid us wel - come, We shall come re - joic - ing,

CHORUS.

bring-ing in the sheaves. Bringing in the sheaves, bringing in the sheaves.

We shall come rejoice- { ing, bringing in the sheaves,
Omit second time. } ing, bringing in the sheaves.

No. 181. Stand for the Right.

*"Stand, therefore, * * * and having done all, stand."*—Eph. 6: 13, 14.

JULIA H. JOHNSTON. J. H. BURKE.

1. Oh! sol - diers of Christ, un - to thee is the call, The
2. The ar - mor of God shall thy weak - ness de - fend, "Be
3. Oh! stand for the right in the face of the foe, Be-

word of com - mand sounds a - loud un - to all, "Be
strong in the faith," and hope on to the end; No
lieve in thy God, and His might He will show; He

strong in the Lord and the power of His might" Be watch-ful and read - y and
le - gions of sin shall thy spir - it af-fright, Be watch-ful and read - y and
leads in the dark, He will keep thee by night, Be watch-ful and read - y and

CHORUS.

stand for the right. Stand for the Right! Stand for the Right!

Stand for the Right. —Concluded.

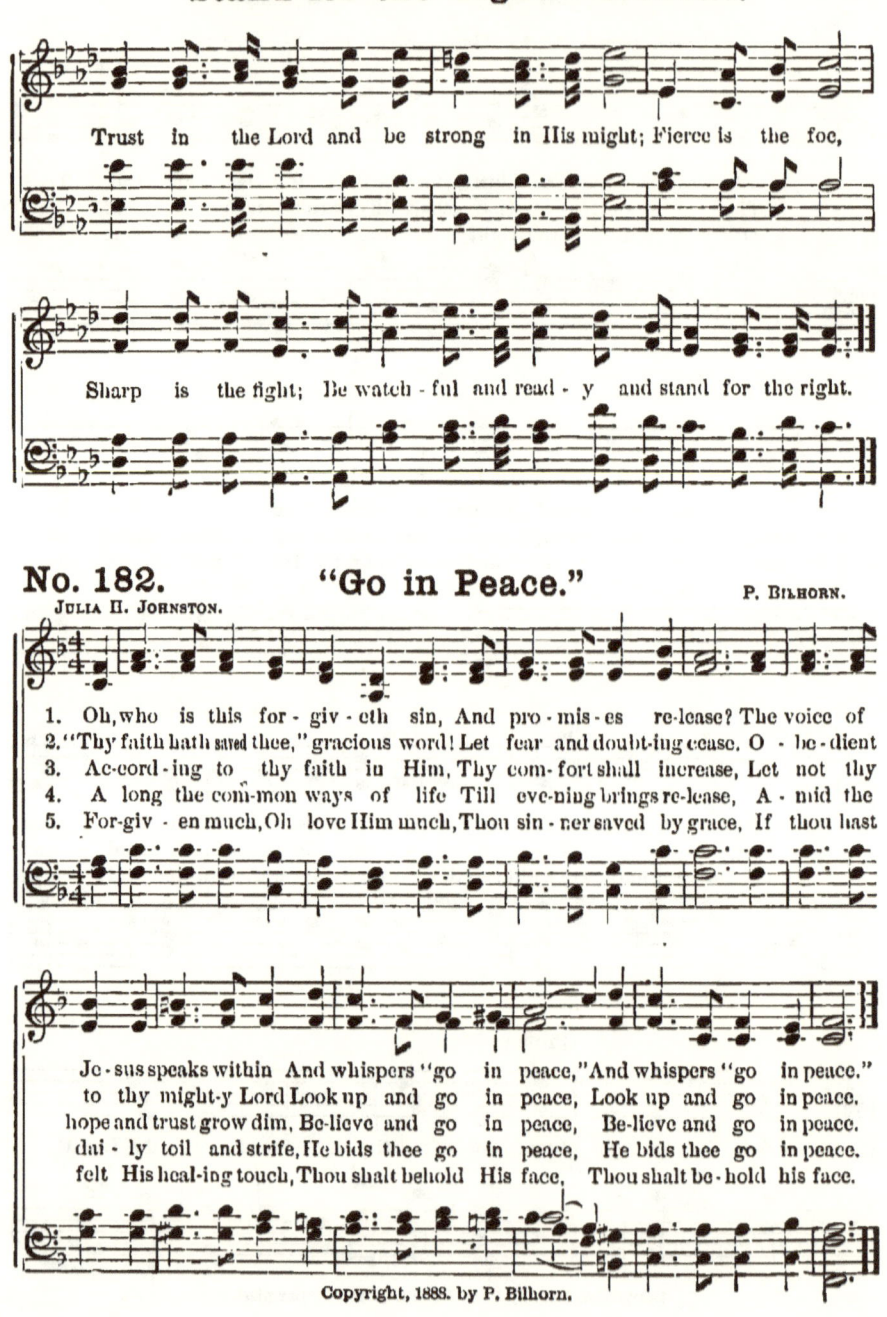

Trust in the Lord and be strong in His might; Fierce is the foe,

Sharp is the fight; Be watch-ful and read-y and stand for the right.

No. 182.   "Go in Peace."   P. Bilhorn.

JULIA H. JOHNSTON.

1. Oh, who is this for-giv-eth sin, And pro-mis-es re-lease? The voice of
2. "Thy faith hath saved thee," gracious word! Let fear and doubt-ing cease. O - be-dient
3. Ac-cord-ing to thy faith in Him, Thy com-fort shall increase, Let not thy
4. A long the com-mon ways of life Till eve-ning brings re-lease, A - mid the
5. For-giv - en much, Oh love Him much, Thou sin - ner saved by grace, If thou hast

Je - sus speaks within And whispers "go in peace,"And whispers "go in peace."
to thy might-y Lord Look up and go in peace, Look up and go in peace.
hope and trust grow dim, Be-lieve and go in peace, Be-lieve and go in peace.
dai - ly toil and strife, He bids thee go in peace, He bids thee go in peace.
felt His heal-ing touch, Thou shalt behold His face, Thou shalt be-hold his face.

No. 183.   Is My Name Written There?

M. A. K.

Frank M. Davis,

1. Lord, I care not for rich-es, Neith-er sil-ver nor gold;
2. Lord, my sins they are man-y, Like the sands of the sea,
3. Oh! that beau-ti-ful cit-y, With its man-sions of light,

I would make sure of heav-en, I would en-ter the fold;
But thy blood, O my Sav-ior, is suf-fi-cient for me;
With its glo-ri-fied be-ings, In pure gar-ments of white;

In the book of Thy king-dom, With its pa-ges so fair,
For Thy prom-ise is writ-ten, In bright let-ters that glow,
Where no e-vil thing com-eth, To de-spoil what is fair;

Tell me, Je-sus, my Sav-ior, Is my name writ-ten there?
"Tho' your sins be as scar-let, They shall be white as snow.
Where the an-gels are watch-ing, Is my name writ-ten there?

Refrain.

Is my name writ-ten there, On the page white and fair?

By permission.

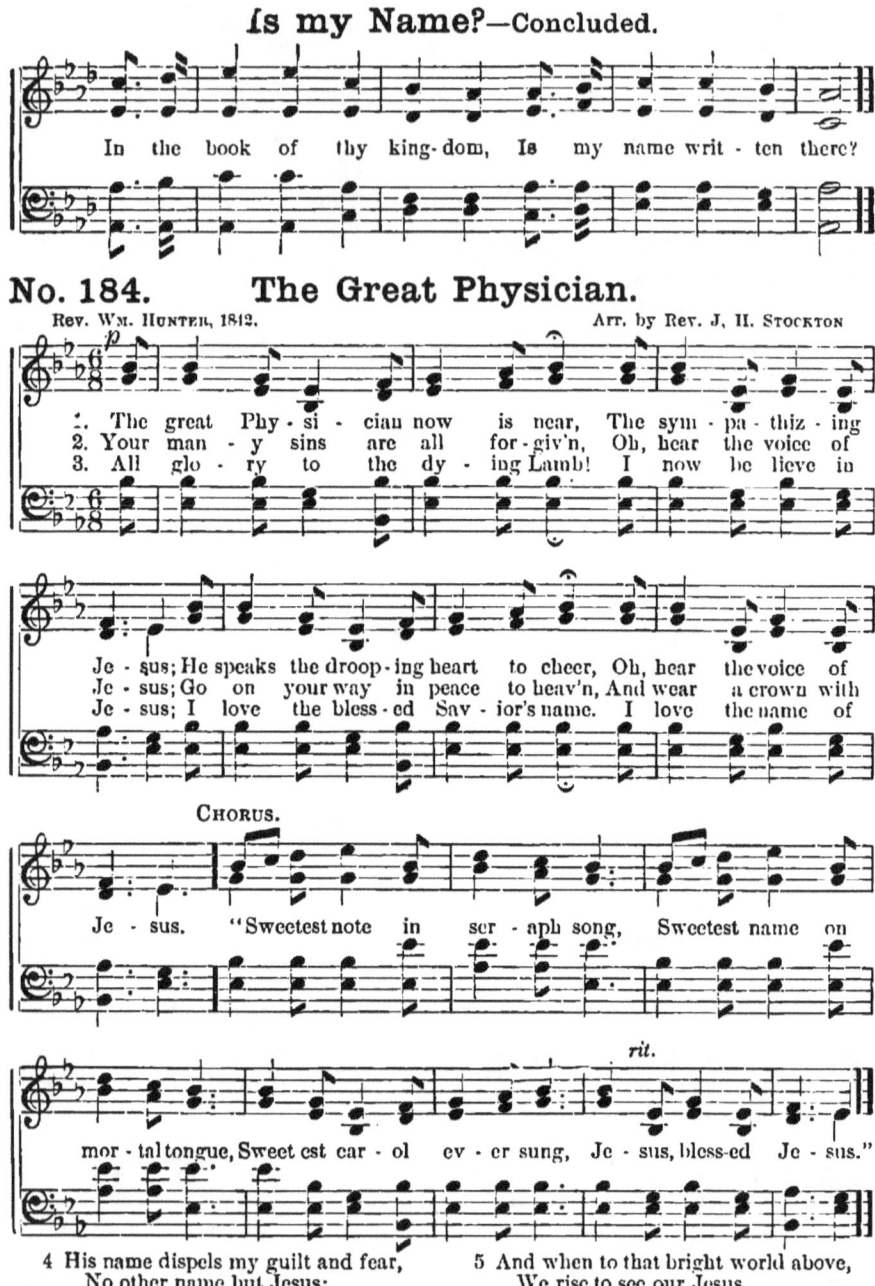

In the book of thy king-dom, Is my name writ-ten there?

No. 184.   The Great Physician.

Rev. WM. HUNTER, 1812.   Arr. by Rev. J. H. STOCKTON

1. The great Phy-si-cian now is near, The sym-pa-thiz-ing
2. Your man-y sins are all for-giv'n, Oh, hear the voice of
3. All glo-ry to the dy-ing Lamb! I now be-lieve in

Je-sus; He speaks the droop-ing heart to cheer, Oh, hear the voice of
Je-sus; Go on your way in peace to heav'n, And wear a crown with
Je-sus; I love the bless-ed Sav-ior's name. I love the name of

CHORUS.

Je-sus. "Sweetest note in ser-aph song, Sweetest name on

rit.

mor-tal tongue, Sweet-est car-ol ev-er sung, Je-sus, bless-ed Je-sus."

4 His name dispels my guilt and fear,
No other name but Jesus;
Oh, how my soul delights to hear
The precious name of Jesus.   **By per.**

5 And when to that bright world above,
We rise to see our Jesus,
We'll sing around the throne of love
His name, the name of Jesus.

No. 185. Give me the Wings of Faith.

" Here we have no continuing city."—HEB. 13 : 14.

Rev. I. WATTS, 1700.　　　　　　　　　　Arr, by WALTER KITTREDGE.

SOLO.

1. Give me the wings of faith to rise, With-in the vail, and see The
2. Once they were mourners here be - low, And pour'd out cries and tears; They
3. I ask them whence their vic - t'ry came: They with u - ni - ted breath, As-

saints a - bove, how great their joys, How bright their glo - ries be.
wres-tled hard, as we do now, With sins, and doubts, and fears,
cribe their con-quest to the Lamb, Their tri - umph to his death.

CHORUS.

Many are the friends who are waiting to-day, Hap-py on the gold-en strand,

Many are the voi - ces call-ing us a-way, To join their glorious band.

Repeat pp

Calling us a-way, Call-ing us a-way, Call-ing to the bet - ter land.

No. 186. How firm a Foundation.

GEORGE KEITH.   PORTUGUESE HYMN.

1. How firm a foun-da-tion, ye saints of the Lord, Is laid for your
2. "Fear not, I am with thee, O be not dis-mayed, For I am thy
3. "When thro' the deep wa-ters I call thee to go, The riv-ers of
4. "The soul that on Je-sus hath leaned for re-pose, I will not, I

faith in his ex - cel-lent word, What more can he say, than to
God, I will still give thee aid; I'll strengthen thee, help thee, and
sor - row shall not o-ver-flow; For I will be with thee the
will not de-sert to his foes; That soul, though all hell should en -

you he hath said, To you, who for re fuge to Je - sus have
cause thee to stand, Up-held by my grac-ious, om-ni - po-tent
tri - als to bless, And sanc-ti-fy to thee thy deep-est dis-
deav - or to shake, I'll nev - er, no nev-er, no nev-er for-

fled? To you, who for re - fuge to Je - sus have fled?
hand, Up-held by my grac-ious, om-ni - po-tent hand."
tress, And sanc-ti-fy to thee thy deep-est dis-tress."
sake, I'll nev-er, no nev-er, no nev-er for-sake!"

No. 187. When our Waiting shall be Over.

Neva E. Parkhill.　　　　　　　　　　　　　　　　　　G. R. Sturgis.

1. When our ea - ger, long-ing spir - its, Furl their wings to take their flight,
2. When there comes the last un - clos - ing Of these wea - ry, ach - ing hands,
3. When the pains of life are van - ish'd, And the new - er sense of peace,
4. O the peace, the joy, the rapt - ure, That is wait - ing us at home,

To the mys - tic shores of beau - ty far a - way, Will the
Will the hearts that mourn for loved ones far a - way, E'er be
Folds us in its ten - der arms of rest for aye, All the
Where the heart for rest, shall nev - er breathe a sigh, O the

bea - con light of glo - ry, Shed its ray of brightness o'er us,
si - lenced in their yearn-ings, Si - lenced in their wist - ful long-ings,
old - en friends a - round us, With the old - en ties that bound us,
song of bliss that's swell - ing, Ev - 'ry tone so sweet - ly tell - ing,

When our wait - ing shall be o - ver by and by.
And a - rise in strength and beau - ty by and by.
Shall we dwell in rest and glad - ness by and by.
We shall rest in love for - ev - er by and by.

By permission.

When our Waiting, etc. Concluded.

No. 188. Deliverance Will Come.

J. B. M.

Rev. J. B. MATTHIAS, 1836.

1. { I saw a way-worn trav-'ler In tat-ter'd gar-ments clad,
   { His back was la-den heav-y, His strength was al-most gone,

2. { The sum-mer sun was shin-ing, The sweat was on his brow,
   { But he kept press-ing on-ward, For he was wend-ing home;

3. { The song-sters in the ar-bor, That stood be-side the way,
   { His watch-word be-ing, "On-ward!" He stopped his ears and ran,

And strug-gling up the moun-tain, It seemed that he was sad; }
Yet he shout-ed as he jour-neyed, De-liv-er-ance will come. }

His gar-ments worn and dust-y, His step seemed ver-y slow; }
Still shout-ing, as he jour-neyed, De-liv-er-ance will come. }

At-tract-ed his at-ten-tion, In-vit-ing his de-lay: }
Still shout-ing, as he jour-neyed, De-liv-er-ance will come. }

CHORUS.

Then palms of vic-to-ry, crowns of glo-ry, Palms of vic-to-ry I shall wear.

4. I saw him in the evening,
   The sun was bending low;
   He overtopped the mountain,
   And reached the vale below:
   He gained the golden city—
   His everlasting home—
   And shouted loud, Hosanna,
   Deliverance has come!

5. I heard the song of triumph
   They sang upon that shore,
   Saying, Jesus has redeemed us
   To suffer nevermore:
   Then, casting his eyes backward
   On the race which he had run,
   He shouted loud, Hosanna,
   The victory has come!

No. 189.　　　　　**Gordon.**

ALFRED BEIRLY.

1. Sovereign of worlds! dis-play thy power, Be this thy Zi - on's fa vored hour;
2. Set up thy throne where Sa - tan reigns, On west-ern wilds and east - ern plains;
3. Speak, and the world shall hear thy voice, Speak, and the des - ert shall re joice;

Oh, bid the morn-ing star a - rise, Oh, point the hea-then to the skies.
Far let the gos - pel's sound be known, Make thou the u - ni verse thine own.
Dis-pel the gloom of hea-then night, Bid ev' - ry na - tion hail the light.

No. 190.　　　　**Sun of my Soul.**

The Lord God is a sun.—Ps. 74: 11.

JOHN KEBLE, 1827.　　　　　　　German. Arr. by W. H. MONK.

1. Sun of my soul, Thou Sav - ior dear, It is not night if Thou be near;
2. When the soft dews of kind - ly sleep, My wea-ried eye - lids gen - tly steep,
3. A - bide with me from morn till eve, For with-out Thee I can - not live;
4. Watch by the sick; en - rich the poor With blessings from thy boundless store;
5. Come near and bless us when we wake, Ere thro' the world our way we take.

Oh, may no earth-born cloud a - rise, To hide Thee from Thy ser-vant's eyes.
Be my last tho't, how sweet to rest For - ev - er on my Sav-ior's breast.
A - bide with me when night is nigh, For with-out Thee I dare not die.
Be ev - 'ry mourn-er's sleep to - night, Like in-fant's slum - bers, pure and light.
Till in the o - cean of Thy love We lose our - selves in heaven a - bove.

No. 191. In the Christian's Home in Glory.

Samuel Young Harmer, 1856.   (John xiv. 2.)   Wm. McDonald, 1856.

1. In the Chris-tian's home in glo - ry There re - mains a land of rest,
2. Pain and sick - ness ne'er shall en - ter, Grief nor woe my lot shall share,
3. Sing, O sing, ye heirs of glo - ry, Shout your tri - umph as you go;

There my Sav - ior's gone be - fore me, To ful - fill my soul's re - quest.
But in that ce - les - tial cen - ter I a crown of life shall wear.
Zi - on's gate will o - pen for you, You shall find an en - trance thro'.

CHORUS.

There is rest for the wea - ry, There is rest for the wea - ry,
On the oth - er side of Jor - dan, In the sweet fields of E - den,

There is rest for the wea - ry, There is rest for you,
Where the tree of life is bloom - ing, There is rest for you.

By permission,

No. 192.
H. BONAR.

What a Friend.

C. C. CONVERSE, By per.

1. What a friend we have in Je-sus, All our sins and griefs to bear!

FINE.

What a priv-i-lege to car-ry Ev-'ry thing to God in prayer!
D.S. All be-cause we do not car-ry Ev-'ry thing to God in prayer!

D.S.

Oh, what peace we of-ten for-feit, Oh, what need-less pain we bear,

2 Have we trials and temptations?
　Is there trouble anywhere?
We should never be discouraged,
　Take it to the Lord in prayer.
Can we find a friend so faithful,
　Who will all our sorrows share?
Jesus knows our every weakness,
　Take it to the Lord in prayer.

3 Are we weak and heavy laden,
　Cumbered with a load of care?
Precious Saviour, still our refuge,—
　Take it to the Lord in prayer.
Do thy friends despise, forsake thee?
　Take it to the Lord in prayer;
In His arms He'll take and shield thee.
　Thou wilt find a solace there.

No. 193.
A. M. TOPLADY.

Rock of Ages.

THOS. HASTINGS.
FINE.

1. Rock of A-ges cleft for me, Let me hide my-self in Thee;
D. C. Be of sin the dou-ble cure, Save from wrath and make me pure.

D.C.

{ Let the wa-ter and the blood,
From Thy wounded side which flow'd, }

2 Could my tears forever flow,
Could my zeal no languor know,
These for sin could not atone;
Thou must save, and Thou alone
In my hand no price I bring;
Simply to thy cross I cling.
3 While I draw this fleeting breath,
When my eyes shall close in death,
When I rise to worlds unknown,
And behold Thee on Thy Throne,
Rock of Ages cleft for me,
Let me hide my self in Thee.

Cross and Crown.

Thomas Sheperd.   Geo. N. Allen.

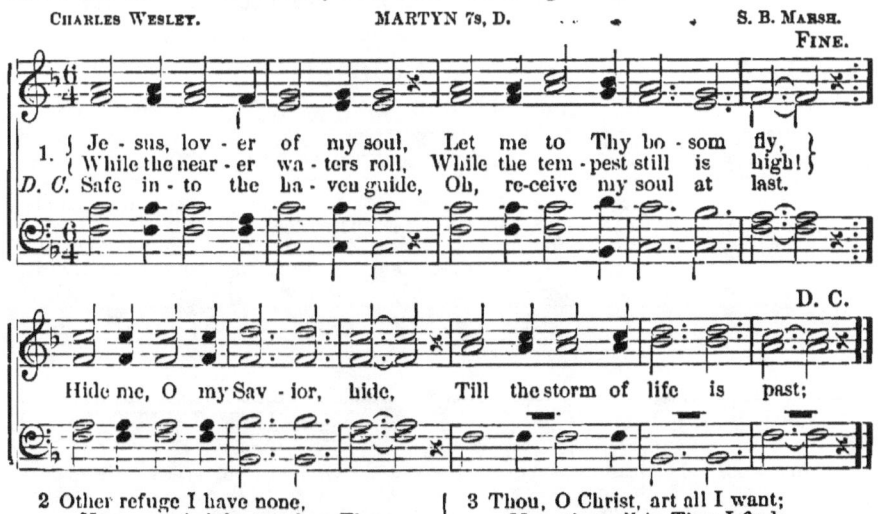

1. Must Je - sus bear the cross a - lone, And all the world go free?
2. The con - se - cra - ted cross I'll bear, Till death shall set me free;
3. O pre - cious cross! O glo - rious crown! O res - ur - rec - tion day!

No, there's a cross for ev - ery one, And there's a cross for me.
And then go home my crown to wear, For there's a crown for me.
Ye au - gels, from the stars come down, And bear my soul a - way.

No. 195.   Jesus, Lover of My Soul.

Charles Wesley.   MARTYN 7s, D.   S. B. Marsh.
                                                             FINE.

1. { Je - sus, lov - er of my soul, Let me to Thy bo - som fly, }
   { While the near - er wa - ters roll, While the tem - pest still is high! }
D. C. Safe in - to the ha - ven guide, Oh, re - ceive my soul at last.

D. C.

Hide me, O my Sav - ior, hide, Till the storm of life is past;

2 Other refuge I have none,
   Hangs my helpless soul on Thee;
Leave, oh leave me not alone,
   Still support and comfort me.
All my trust on Thee is stayed,
   All my help from Thee I bring;
Cover my defenceless head
   With the shadow of Thy wing.

3 Thou, O Christ, art all I want;
   More than all in Thee I find;
Raise the fallen! cheer the faint!
   Heal the sick! and lend the blind!
Just and holy is Thy Name,
   I am all unrighteousness:
Vile and full of sin I am,
   Thou art full of truth and grace.

No. 196. Just as I Am.

CHARLOTTE ELLIOTT.　　WOODWORTH. L. M.　　WM. B. BRADBURY.

1. Just as I am, with-out one plea, But that Thy blood was shed for me,
2. Just as I am, and wait-ing not To rid my soul of one dark blot,
3. Just as I am, tho' tossed a-bout, With many a con-flict, many a doubt,

And that Thou bidd'st me come to Thee, O Lamb of God I come, I come!
To Thee, whose blood can cleanse each spot, O Lamb of God I come, I come!
Fightings and fears with-in, without, O Lamb of God I come, I come!

4 Just as I am, poor, wretched, blind,
Sight, riches, healing of the mind,
Yea, all I need in Thee to find,
O Lamb of God! I come, I come!

5 Just as I am; Thou wilt receive,
Wilt welcome, pardon, cleanse, relieve;
Because Thy promise I believe,
O Lamb of God! I come, I come!

No. 197. Am I a Soldier.

ISAAC WATTS.　　ARLINGTON. C.M.　　THOS. A. ARNE.

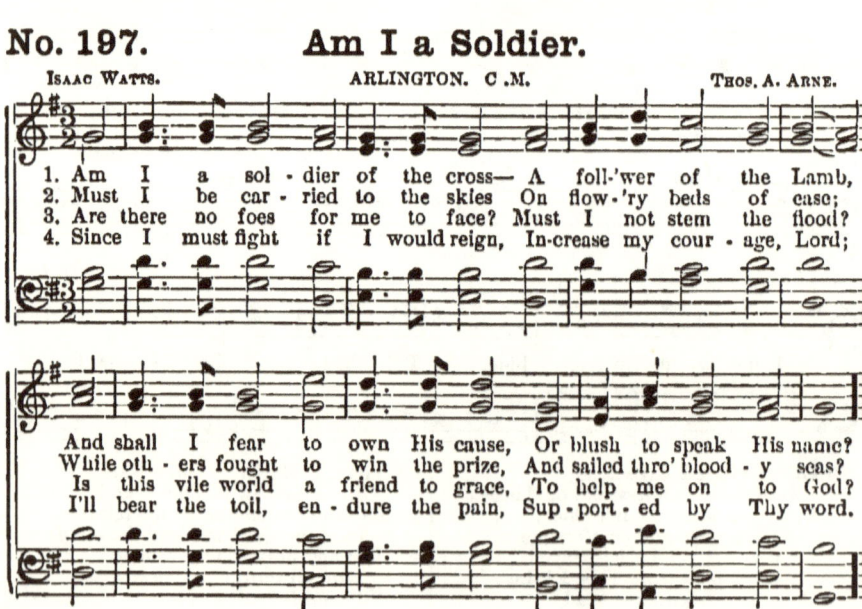

1. Am I a sol-dier of the cross— A foll-'wer of the Lamb,
2. Must I be car-ried to the skies On flow-'ry beds of ease;
3. Are there no foes for me to face? Must I not stem the flood?
4. Since I must fight if I would reign, In-crease my cour-age, Lord;

And shall I fear to own His cause, Or blush to speak His name?
While oth-ers fought to win the prize, And sailed thro' blood-y seas?
Is this vile world a friend to grace, To help me on to God?
I'll bear the toil, en-dure the pain, Sup-port-ed by Thy word.

No. 198. Blest be the Tie.

Rev. JOHN FAWCETT.   DENNIS.   From H. G. NAGELI.

1. Blest be the tie that binds Our hearts in Christ-ian love,
2. Be - fore our Fa - ther's throne, We pour our ar - dent pray'rs;
3. We share our mut - ual woes; Our mut - ual bur - dens bear;
4. When we a - sun - der part, It gives us in - ward pain;

The fel - low - ship of kin - dred minds is like to that a - bove.
Our fears, our hopes, our aims are one.—Our com - forts and our cares.
And of - ten for each oth - er flows The sym - pa - thiz - ing tear.
But we shall still be join'd in heart, And hope to meet a - gain.

No. 199. Come, Thou Fount.

Rev. R. ROBINSON, 1758.   NETTLETON.   Old Melody, 1812.

FINE.

1. Come, Thou Fount of ev - ery bless - ing, Tune my heart to sing Thy grace;
   Streams of mer - cy, nev - er ceas - ing, Call for songs of loud-est praise;
D. C. Praise the mount, I'm fixed up - on it! Mount of Thy re - deeming love.

D. C.

Teach me some me - lo-dious son-net, Sung by flam - ing tongues a-bove;

2 Here I'll raise my Ebenezer,
    Hither by Thy help I'm come;
And I hope by Thy good pleasure,
    Safely to arrive at home.
Jesus sought me when a stranger,
    Wandering from the fold of God;
He to rescue me from danger
    Interposed His precious blood.

3 Oh, to grace how great a debtor,
    Daily I'm constrained to be!
Let Thy goodness as a fetter,
    Bind my wandering heart to Thee;
Prone to wander, Lord, I feel it—
    Prone to leave the God I love—
Here's my heart, oh, take and seal it,
    Seal it for Thy courts above.

No. 200. Come ye that Love the Lord.

Words by Isaac Watts.—Arranged.

Arranged.

1. Come ye that love the Lord, And let your joys be known;
Cho. I'm glad sal-va-tion's free, I'm glad sal va-tion's free;

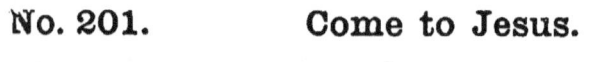

Join in a song with sweet ac-cord, While ye sur-round His throne.
Sal-va-tion's free for you and me; I'm glad sal-va-tion's free.

2 Let those refuse to sing
   Who never knew our God,
But servants of the heavenly King
   May speak His praise abroad.—Cho.

3 Then let our songs abound,
   And every tear be dry;
We're marching thro' Immanuel's ground,
   To fairer worlds on high.—Cho

No. 201. Come to Jesus.

1. Come to Je-sus, Come to Je-sus, Come to Je-sus just now;

Just now Come to Je-sus, Come to Je-sus just now.

2. He will save you.	7. Call upon Him.	12. Only trust Him.
3. Oh, believe Him,	8. He will hear you.	13. Jesus loves you.
4. He is able.	9. Look unto Him.	14. Don't reject Him.
5. He is willing.	10. He'll forgive you.	15. I believe Him.
6. He'll receive you.	11. Flee to Jesus.	16. Hallelujah. Amen.

No. 202. Sweet Hour of Prayer.

1

Sweet hour of prayer, sweet hour of prayer,
That calls me from a world of care,
And bids me at my Father's throne
Make all my wants and wishes known!
In seasons of distress and grief
My soul has often found relief,
And oft escaped the tempter's snare
By thy return, sweet hour of prayer.

2

Sweet hour of prayer, sweet hour of prayer,
Thy wings shall my petition bear
To Him, whose truth and faithfulness
Engage the waiting soul to bless:
And since he bids me seek His face,
Believe His word, and trust His grace,
I'll cast on Him my every care,
And wait for thee, sweet hour of prayer.

No. 203. Over There.

1

O think of the home over there,
By the side of the river of light,
Where the saints all immortal and fair,
Are robed in the garments of white.

2

Oh, think of the friends over there,
Who before us the journey have trod,
Of the songs that they breathe on the air
In their homes in the palace of God.

3

I'll soon be at home over there,
For the end of my journey I see;
Many dear to my heart, over there,
Are watching and waiting for me.

No. 204. Even Me.

1 Lord, I hear of showers of blessing
  Thou art scattering full and free;
  Showers, the thirsty land refreshing;
  Let some drops now fall on me,
    Even me.

2 Pass me not, O God, my Father,
  Sinful though my heart may be;
  Thou might'st leave me, but the rather
  Let Thy mercy light on me.
    Even me.

3 Pass me not, O gracious Savior,
  Let me live and cling to thee;
  I am longing for Thy favor;
  Whilst Thou'rt calling, O call me,
    Even me.

No. 205. He Leadeth Me.

1 He leadeth me! oh, blessed thought,
  Oh, words with heavenly comfort fraught,
  Whate'er I do, where'er I be,
  Still 'tis God's hand that leadeth me!

Cho.—He leadeth me, He leadeth me,
  By His own hand He leadeth me;
  His faithful follower I would be,
  For by His hand He leadeth me.

2 Sometimes mid scenes of deepest gloom,
  Sometimes where Eden's bowers bloom,
  By waters still, o'er troubled sea,—
  Still 'tis God's hand that leadeth me.

3 Lord, I would clasp Thy hand in mine,
  Nor ever murmur nor repine,
  Content, whatever lot I see,
  Since 'tis my God that leadeth me.

No 206. At The Fountain.

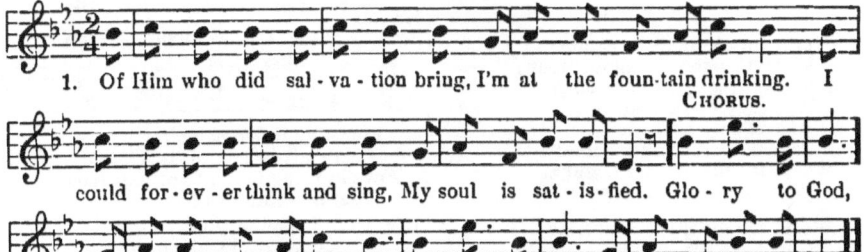

1. Of Him who did sal-va-tion bring, I'm at the foun-tain drinking. I
CHORUS.
could for-ev-er think and sing, My soul is sat-is-fied. Glo-ry to God,
I'm at the foun-tain drink-ing, Glo-ry to God, My soul is sat-is-fied.

2

Ask but His grace, and lo! 'tis given,
  I'm at the fountain drinking,
Ask and He turns your hell to heaven,
  I'm on my journey home.

3

Tho' sin and sorrow wound my soul,
  I'm at the fountain drinking,
Jesus, Thy balm will make me whole,
  I'm on my journey home.

Nearer, My God, to Thee.

1 Nearer, my God, to Thee;
   Nearer to Thee;
E'en though it be a cross,
   That raiseth me,
Still all my song shall be,
|:Nearer, my God, to thee,:|
   Nearer to Thee,

2 Though like the wanderer,
   The sun gone down,
Darkness be over me,
   My rest a stone,
Yet in my dreams I'd be
|:Nearer, my God, to thee,:|
   Nearer to Thee.

3 There let the way appear,
   Steps unto heaven;
All that Thou sendest me,
   In mercy given;
Angels to beckon me
|:Nearer, my God, to Thee,:|
   Nearer to thee.

No. 208.
Work, for the Night is Coming.

1 Work, for the night is coming,
   Work, through the morning hours;
Work, while the dew is sparkling,
   Work, 'mid springing flowers;
Work, when the day grows brighter,
   Work in the glowing sun;
Work, for the night is coming,
   When man's work is done.

2 Work, for the night is coming,
   Work through the sunny noon;
Fill brightest hours with labor,
   Rest comes sure and soon,
Give every flying minute,
   Something to keep in store;
Work, for the night is coming,
   When man works no more.

3 Work, for the night is coming,
   Under the sunset skies;
While the bright tints are glowing,
   Work, for the daylight flies,
Work till the last beam fadeth,
   Fadeth to shine no more;
Work while the night is darkening,
   When man's work is o'er.

No. 209.
There is a Fountain

1 There is a fountain filled with blood,
   Drawn from Immanuel's veins;
And sinners plunged beneath that flood,
   Lose all their guilty stains.

2 The dying thief rejoiced to see
   That fountain in his day;
And there may I though vile as he,
   Wash all my sins away.

3 Then in a nobler, sweet song,
   I'll sing Thy power to save,
When this poor lisping, stammering tongue
   Lies silent in the grave.

No. 210.
I am Coming to the Cross.

1 I am coming to the cross,
   I am poor, and weak, and blind;
I am counting all but dross,
   I shall full salvation find.

   Cho.—I am trusting Lord, in Thee,
      Blest Lamb of Calvary;
      Humbly at Thy cross I bow,
      Jesus saves, He saves me now,

2 Long my heart has sighed for Thee,
   Long has evil reigned within;
Jesus sweetly speaks to me,—
   "I will cleanse you from all sin."—Cho.

3 Here I give my all to Thee,
   Friends, and time, and earthly store;
Soul and body Thine to be,—
   Wholly Thine for evermore.—Cho.

4 Jesus comes! He fills my soul!
   Perfected in Him I am;
I am every whit made whole:
   Glory, glory to the Lamb.—Cho.

No. 211.
I Hear Thy Welcome Voice.

1 I hear Thy welcome voice,
   That calls me, Lord, to Thee,
For cleansing in Thy precious blood,
   That flowed on Calvary.

Cho.—I am coming, Lord,
      Coming now to Thee!
      Wash me, cleanse me in the blood,
   That flowed on Calvary.

2 Though coming weak and vile,
   Thou dost my strength assure;
Thou dost my vileness fully cleanse,
   Till spotless all and pure.

No. 212. **Doxology.**

Words by SAMUEL DAVIES. SESSIONS. Music by L. O. EMERSON.

Praise God from whom all blessings flow; Praise Him, all creatures here be-low;

Praise Him a - bove, ye heavenly host, Praise Father, Son and Ho - ly Ghost.

No. 213. **Old Hundred. L. M.**

Bp. THOS. KEN. 1697. G. FRANC.

Praise God, from whom all blessings flow; Praise Him, all crea-tures here be-low;

Praise Him a - bove, ye heav'n-ly host; Praise Father, Son, and Ho - ly Ghost.

No. 214. **Gloria Patri.**

1. Glory be to the Father, and to the Son, and to the Ho - ly Ghost;
2. As it was in the begin-ning, is now, and ev - er shall be, world with - out end. A - men.

INDEX.

Titles in Romans. *First Lines in Italics.*